SNOWED IN WITH THE RELUCTANT TYCOON

SNOWED IN WITH THE RELUCTANT TYCOON

NINA SINGH

MILLS & BOON

First published in Great Britain 2017
by Mills & Boon, an imprint of HarperCollins*Publishers*
1 London Bridge Street, London, SE1 9GF

Large Print edition 2018

© 2017 Nilay Nina Singh

ISBN: 978-0-263-07360-7

MIX
Paper from
responsible sources
FSC
www.fsc.org   FSC® C007454

This book is produced from independently certified
FSC™ paper to ensure responsible forest management.
For more information visit www.harpercollins.co.uk/green.

Printed and bound in Great Britain
by CPI Group (UK) Ltd, Croydon, CR0 4YY

To my mother and father. For all their faith.

CHAPTER ONE

THE HOUSE WAS COLD.

Carli Tynan wasn't surprised. In fact, she'd never once entered this mansion and ever felt warm. Regardless of the season. And, despite the myriad of Christmas decorations currently adorning the foyer, nothing about the home felt particularly festive. Or even like a home. No, the Hammond estate felt more like a staid museum.

The eleven-foot-tall pine Christmas tree that nearly touched the ceiling notwithstanding.

Shaking the thin layer of snow off her wool coat, she peeled off her faux leather gloves, the bound portfolio tucked under her right arm. The darn portfolio was the only reason she was here, the reason her usual morning routine had been so handily disrupted. Carli was not a fan of disruptions. She'd already had to deal with way too many in her twenty-six years.

Her boss, Jackson Hammond, had asked her

just this morning to drop off the file on her way in to work. Right after she'd gotten back from her early-morning run. It had barely given her time to shower, let alone to put herself together as well as she normally liked. As a result, her unruly curls were now a mess of tangles hastily secured in a haphazard bun on top of her head. She hadn't even had a chance to iron her remaining clean suit. The only other option was a stretch pencil dress that had recently shrunk after she'd accidently thrown it in the dryer. Comfortable, it was not.

But she had a day full of meetings in the office, and this was the best she could do. Not at all the way she would have preferred to start off her morning. Or any morning for that matter.

All because the prodigal son was returning home.

Justin Hammond, Jackson's second-born, had been the one to request the portfolio. And apparently, he needed it before he could make it into the office. Carli had to accommodate him. Why was he suddenly heading back into town anyway? Justin hadn't had anything to do with Hammond's Toys since she'd been employed there.

Now, suddenly, he was interested. Carli stepped farther into the foyer and couldn't resist the urge to roll her eyes. No doubt Justin's sudden interest was due to his older brother James's recent distractions, so to speak. James had apparently met someone and was now taking a well-deserved break from the day-to-day business. Little brother must have concluded that this was an ideal time to strike.

Never mind that Carli should be the one next in line to take over any of the duties James may be ready to relinquish. She couldn't help but feel a little insulted.

And hurt. Well, she'd just have to get over it. Then she'd have to work even harder to ensure she got the position she deserved.

She walked up to the foot of the stairs and yelled up toward the second floor. "Mr. Hammond, I'm dropping off the file."

No answer.

Jackson's hearing wasn't what it used to be. She shrugged off her coat and dropped it on the nearby black leather settee, then walked halfway up the grand spiral stairway.

"Mr. Hammond, where would you like the files?"

Again, nothing. Carli let out a huff of frustration. She certainly didn't want to risk having come out here only to have the portfolio overlooked because the Hammond men couldn't find it. She would have texted Jackson, but he was notorious for wanting to have nothing to do with technology. He probably didn't even look at his phone every day. Hence the request for a paper file. As for Justin Hammond, she barely knew a thing about him, let alone his cell phone number.

She walked all the way up to the hallway and toward Mr. Hammond's suite. The shower was running. Great. She would have to yell through the door at the top of her lungs, or he would never hear her.

Could this morning get any worse? She didn't think so.

Stepping into the master suite, she walked over to Mr. Hammond's antique mahogany desk and dropped the portfolio atop it. Then yelled as loud as she dared across the room toward the closed master bathroom door. "The portfolio is on your desk, Mr. Hammond."

A muffled acknowledgment sounded from the other side, and Carli breathed a sigh of relief. Now she could get out of here and finally start her day.

But the day had other plans. When she was midway down the stairs, the front door opened and a shadowy, tall figure stepped into the foyer. He dropped his suitcase to the floor and seemed to hesitate before entering any farther. Carli's step nearly faltered as she took in the sight of him. Tall and dark with a firm square jaw and jet-black hair. There was no mistaking who he was—Justin, the other Hammond heir. All three men shared the same rugged features, but the one standing before her had a different vibe altogether. An aura she would be hard-pressed to describe.

Regaining her balance, she managed to finally make her way down the stairs.

Justin finally looked up as she reached the foyer. He seemed to do a double take. Most men did when they first got a look at her. A fact she was quite aware of. And quite uncomfortable with.

"I'm sorry," he began, though he looked anything but. "I didn't realize anyone was here." He looked downright annoyed.

She tried to summon a polite smile, but her facial muscles seemed useless. Justin Hammond had eyes that a sorcerer would envy. The lightest shade of hazel littered with gold specks. What was wrong with her? She so wasn't the type to notice men's eyes, for heaven's sake.

"Um, your father's in the shower. I'm sure he'll be right out." In an awkward attempt to introduce herself, she extended her right hand. "I'm Car—"

But he stopped her midsentence. "Look, that's hardly necessary."

Carli blinked. Okay. No time for a quick introduction? Maybe he was just jet-lagged and tired from travel. Or perhaps he was just plain rude.

She cleared her throat. "Oh, I guess—" She looked to the side, unable to bear his gaze much longer given the awkwardness. "I guess I'll be on my way then."

He merely nodded, then stepped aside.

Carli tried not to flinch. She'd just effectively been shown the door! By the man who threatened the job she'd been working so hard for, no less.

Straightening to her full height, Carli stepped

around him and went to grab her coat from the settee. Then did the only thing she could. She left.

Her words about the morning not getting any worse mocked her.

Justin watched as the woman walked out and firmly shut the door behind her. Perhaps he'd been on the slim side of rude just now, but he so hadn't been expecting a stunning bombshell to come down the stairs as he entered his boyhood home. Not that he'd really been expecting anything in particular after having been gone over two decades.

Looked like his father's womanizing ways hadn't changed.

He glanced out the side palladium window as the woman walked down the driveway toward the parked car outside. *Ravishing*. It was the only word that came to mind. She had curves that would stop a monk in his tracks. The dress she wore hugged those curves in all the right ways. His father apparently liked them much younger these days; she had to be barely in her late twenties.

Well, it was no business of his. He was only

here for a few days to analyze some numbers his father wanted him to look at. Though why the old man suddenly requested his younger son's help after all these years was a mystery, one Justin had no interest in investigating. He'd been ready to turn down the request and tell his father where he could go, but his mother had insisted he do Jackson Hammond's bidding. The old man still held the purse strings after all. And his mother had always been all about the Hammond purse strings.

Even after she'd fled this house and his father all those years ago, taking their younger son, him, along with her. He'd been the lucky one to get whisked away in the middle of the night once his mother finally decided she'd had enough.

He hadn't been back since. Until today.

Justin tried to get his bearings as he examined the foyer he hadn't walked through since he'd been a small child. Everything appeared smaller. The traditional Christmas decorations were as spectacular as he remembered. The tall pine by the stairs glittered with gold and silver ornaments. Sparkling lights adorned the stairs and banisters, a line of poinsettias graced the walls.

So festive. In a nauseating and annoying way. All that was missing was a background track of loud Christmas music.

Bah, humbug.

What was he doing here? He should have refused his parents' requests and the hell with the consequences. Who did they think he was? Who did his father think *he* was? This was the same man who had ignored him until his older and rightful heir had decided last month that he'd needed some time off to go do…whatever he was doing. Justin had no idea, but it probably involved a woman. Maybe his brother had fallen in love.

Yeah, right, Justin thought as he made his way toward the living room. He sincerely doubted it. The Hammond genes weren't really conducive to such things. Love wasn't in their DNA.

More Christmas decorations greeted him in the living room, which had been updated with new furniture in addition to a slightly less dark shade of green painted on the walls. Or perhaps that had been the same color all along. He'd been gone from home a long time. Not that it ever really felt like a home to begin with.

Overall, reentering his childhood house so far

felt somewhat surreal. Like he'd stepped into a previous life.

The sound of footsteps coming down the stairs pulled him out of his musings. Steeling himself against the anger barely contained under the surface, Justin turned to face Jackson Hammond— the man who had watched a young Justin being yanked out that front door all those years ago without lifting a finger to stop it.

Past history, Justin thought as he turned to greet his father. Or more accurately, the man who had sired him.

To his surprise, Jackson hadn't changed all that much. The graying at his temples had spread through to most of his thick, wavy hair. A few more wrinkles framed the area around his mouth. Other than that, Justin felt as if he could be looking at the same face he had last seen all those years ago.

"Thank you for coming, son," his father said, and extended a hand. It was the most awkward handshake Justin had ever performed.

"You're welcome."

"I know what a busy man you are, so I really appreciate it."

Justin merely nodded. No need for Jackson to know that if it weren't for his mother's insistence, Justin would still be on the other side of the country.

"Given your global reputation as a management consultant, I figured it was about time you did a full assessment of the company you're part heir to," his father added, then shook his head as if in disbelief. "Something I should have requested long ago."

"I suppose that makes sense," Justin offered.

"You've accomplished quite a lot for such a young age," Jackson added. "That consulting firm of yours is known all over the world." Was that a look of pride on his face? If so, it was too little, and much too late.

"Business has been good."

"So I've read. As well as reading about your fast rise in the industry."

Justin processed his father's words. Words that would have meant the world to him when he was a teenager, or even a college student. How many school events or sporting events had he desperately searched the audience on some small glimmer of hope that Jackson might have shown up?

How many times had the phone rang on his birthday with none of the calls being from his father?

No. Justin had long ago stopped pining for any acknowledgment from the man standing before him. "Why don't I get started then?" he prompted, changing the subject.

What had Jackson expected? If his father had any notion that this visit was to be a touching reunion between long-lost father and son, he was in for a disappointment.

Carli found herself becoming more and more annoyed as she drove away from the Hammond mansion. Of all the nerve! She'd never been dismissed by anyone in such a fashion—and she'd grown up in a houseful of siblings. Undivided attention wasn't exactly something she was used to. But the way Justin Hammond had just practically ejected her had been downright insulting. To make matters worse, she'd done nothing but stood there like a stunned doe. How pathetic.

She took the curve around the next bend a little too fast and realized she was letting her anger get the best of her. Deep breaths. So what if her new boss was a rude, insensitive clod? She could handle it.

He would not get to her. She'd worked too hard and overcome too much to get to where she was in her career. Her job with Hammond's Toys meant everything. And she was good at it, damn it!

Why did Justin Hammond have to show up and put all of it in jeopardy? But there was an even bigger question, she had to admit. Why hadn't she stood up for herself? It was like she'd looked into his eyes and gone totally mute. Recalling his gaze just now had her drawing in a deep breath. Heavens, those caramel-hued eyes were the devil's tool for distraction. And there was something behind them, a distant, haunted look if she'd ever seen one.

She hmmphed. Now she was just getting fanciful. He was just her new boss. And she had to deal with him, that's all.

The honk of a horn behind her startled her out of her thoughts. She'd stopped at a red light and hadn't even noticed it had turned. Time to get a grip.

Justin Hammond had already taken way too much of her time, and she had things to do.

That reminder became all too evident when she made her way into her office. Her assistant was already there at the desk, with a file of papers waiting for Carli's signature or attention. The latest cost-cutting initiative was becoming quite the project—one she'd been given the primary responsibility for. Until Justin was called in, that was.

"Hey, Jocelyn. Sorry I'm late."

The petite brunette gave her a friendly smile. "Don't sweat it. You're not that late."

"Well, it's late for me."

"Please tell me it's because you had a hot, steamy date last night that turned into a wild night. And that he wouldn't let you get up out of bed this morning."

"Last night was a Tuesday."

Jocelyn gave her a blank look. "What's your point?"

Why did she bother? "Never mind. Are those the latest data points?"

Her assistant nodded and handed her the thick

pile of folders. "I printed them like you requested. The electronic file is in your inbox."

"Thanks. You know where I'll be for most of the morning. These numbers are going to take a while to get through. And I'm already behind." *Due to an unexpected project I was just given this morning,* she added to herself. A project for the sole purpose of getting Justin Hammond up to speed on the latest business figures.

"Well, you can't be working on them all morning."

Carli lifted an eyebrow. "Why's that?"

"Mr. Hammond just called and asked me to schedule yet one more meeting. We have an unexpected guest coming in."

Oh, no. Carli could venture to guess who it might be. "Please tell me it's not Justin Hammond."

Jocelyn gave her a curious smile. "I could do that. But I'd be lying to you."

Great. Just great. Was the man sent here just to vex her at every turn? Apparently, she was supposed to jump whenever Justin Hammond needed anything.

Jocelyn studied her, the amused smile still on her face. "Something wrong?"

Carli tried to shake off the frustration. "I just have a lot to do. And he happens to be the reason I'm late to begin with."

"Aha! So I was right."

"Right about what?"

"You were indeed late because of a sexy man."

Jocelyn just didn't know when to let up. "Only because I had to prepare a report for him at the last minute and then deliver it before I got in today."

Her assistant waved her hand in dismissal. "Details."

"Honestly, Jocelyn. I barely met the man for a few scant moments."

"So tell me. Is he as handsome as he appears in all the photos?"

"I didn't notice."

That earned her a disbelieving look. "See. This is why I worry about you. Justin Hammond is one of the most eligible bachelors on the planet. He's on the celebrity sites weekly. Wealthy, successful and handsome. And you didn't even notice his looks?"

"Not really, no." She could fib quite well when she had to.

Jocelyn slammed her hands on her hips. "That's just disappointing. Most of the female staff around here are breathless with anticipation at his arrival. And you act like it's an ordinary day. You gotta give me something. Some small detail I can throw to them."

"That's just silly. He's just the other Hammond heir."

"Right. A mere handsome millionaire who not only has claim to half the largest retail toy company in North America but also made gobs of money on his own."

She did have a point there. Justin's life story so far was a bit on the exceptional side. She was about to begrudgingly admit to that when a small commotion outside her door drew both their attention. Looked like Jocelyn was about to find out firsthand what she was so curious about. Justin had arrived. And he was causing quite a stir, no doubt with most of the female staff. Carli heard "can I get you anything, Mr. Hammond" more than once.

Jocelyn jumped to the door. "Ooh, he's here."

She gasped. "And he's heading right to your office."

A strange sensation spread through Carli's chest. Despite seeing several photos of him throughout the years, she had to admit he wasn't what she'd been expecting. All the pictures hadn't really done him justice. They hadn't captured the soft, tawny hue of his eyes. Or the way his hair fell sloppily over his forehead. She hadn't realized she'd noticed so much of him during those brief moments in the Hammond foyer earlier.

A quick knock on the door, and then Justin stepped into her office. He blinked in surprise when he saw her. "You?"

What was that supposed to mean? Did he want her out already? Genuine surprise registered on his face. Was he here to lay claim to her office, having expected her to vacate it for him already?

Too stunned to speak, Carli was relieved when Jocelyn stepped up to him. "Mr. Hammond, I'm Jocelyn Sumner. We weren't expecting you so early. The meeting isn't until nine thirty."

He hadn't taken his eyes off Carli. She resisted the urge to look away from the intense stare.

"I figured I'd get started," he answered Jocelyn. "I'm looking for the person who put this together." He held up the file of papers Carli dropped off less than an hour ago. "I was told this is their office."

Carli finally found her tongue. "It is."

He blinked at her. "Can you tell me where to find him now?"

Him. "You have," she answered, deliberately omitting further clarification. Let him hang in the wind a bit.

He lifted an eyebrow.

"I'm the one who put it together. I was dropping it off this morning when we…met." She added some emphasis on the last word.

Justin's eyes grew wide as understanding clearly dawned. Jocelyn stood between them, her gaze switching back and forth as if she were watching an exciting tennis game.

Justin cleared his throat. "You did this?" he asked, indicating the file in his hand. "It's, uh, very thorough. Very impressive."

Carli tried not to bristle at his surprised tone. How very insulting. This man didn't know a thing about her. But he'd made his initial judgment already. She wasn't surprised. Men like Justin always came to the most obvious conclusion when it came to her.

How disappointing that he was so typical.

CHAPTER TWO

GREAT, JUSTIN THOUGHT as the woman across the room shot daggers at him. He hadn't realized this morning that she worked for the company. He'd managed to offend one of Hammond's employees on his first day back in town. No, make that his first *hour* back.

She crossed her arms in front of her chest. "Well, you needn't look so surprised. I'm a project manager at Hammond. I can put together a business report."

"That's not what I meant." But what was she doing coming down from his father's suite at that hour? He couldn't be blamed for having jumped to the most obvious conclusion. And he still wasn't sure he was totally wrong. But clearly there was more to the circumstances. "I'm just surprised to see you here, that's all."

"This is my office. Of course, I'm here."

"Not here, in this room. Here at the company."

She merely quirked an eyebrow. A gesture that seemed to add a haughty quality to her features. Her almond-shaped eyes were a deep chocolate brown. Several tendrils of hair escaped her tight bun and framed an olive-shaped face.

Not classically beautiful, but she was striking in an unusual and rare way.

And her figure—he didn't even want to go there.

"Never mind," she declared, and stepped around her desk. "My name is Carli Tynan. I'm regional project manager for Hammond Retail. James hired me, but I work more closely with Jackson."

He reached his hand out to shake hers just as she said, "You, of course, need no introduction."

Her tone suggested she didn't mean that in a complimentary way. "Nice to meet you."

She pointed to the file he still held. "Is there anything you'd like to go over?" This woman was all business. Regardless of what she'd been doing at the mansion earlier, he had no doubt she was an efficient employee who clearly had things under control.

"I made a few notes, things that I wouldn't mind some further clarification on."

She indicated the chair in front of her desk. "Have a seat. We have some time before the meeting."

Justin hesitated. He wasn't used to being ordered around; the feeling made him uncomfortable. As did the incessant echo of Christmas music playing in the lobby.

"Would you mind if we closed the door?" he asked her, already walking to it.

"Any particular reason?"

"I can't focus with the cursed Christmas tunes playing in the background."

He shut the door and turned back to find her studying him with curious eyes. "You have something against Christmas music?"

"Christmas is one day. But for some reason the whole world is burdened with listening to those blasted tunes for weeks on end. That doesn't happen with any other holiday, now does it?"

"Christmas is hardly like any other holiday."

"Only because the whole world insists on dragging it out. It's one day, yet we insist on calling it the holiday season."

"Some would argue it's at least twelve days," she countered.

Clever, she'd referenced another Christmas carol. "Don't tell me you're one of those types. The ones who make their shopping list in October. You pull out the tree and decorations as soon as the Thanksgiving turkey is consumed. Am I close?"

"And what would be so wrong about it if I was?"

He shrugged. He wasn't going to try to explain it. Christmastime around his house as a young boy had usually meant the start of weeks of arguments followed by loud, drunken fights. With his father working long hours and his mother growing more and more resentful at his absence. Of course, there were problems throughout the year, but the holiday season seemed to bring out the worst in his parents. An excuse to purge their anger and throw everything in the open. By the time Christmas morning rolled around, he and his brother were more than ready to have it all over with. Even the toys weren't enough to make up for the turmoil and chaos.

How had they even gotten into this conversation anyway? Justin wondered. All he'd asked was to shut the door so he didn't have to hear the music from the lobby. He didn't need to explain himself to a woman he'd just met.

Carli was still staring at him expectedly. She'd asked him a question that he'd left hanging. "Nothing. Never mind. Forget I said anything."

"Okay. But I feel I have to say just one more thing."

Why was he not surprised? "Go ahead."

"That you have to realize how—" she paused and glanced at the ceiling, as if scrambling for the correct word "—curious your perspective about Christmas is. Given who you are."

Of course he realized that. He was heir to one of the most successful retail toy operations in the Northern Hemisphere. A business that earned most of its profits in the weeks between Thanksgiving and Christmas Eve. Sure, it was true that as an adult he'd made his own way and had become a successful businessman in his own right. But he'd been granted worldly advantages at birth that most people could only dream of. He should be thanking his lucky stars for the gift of Christmas and the commercialism that surrounded it.

And to anyone on the outside, he probably sounded like an ungrateful, cranky Scrooge who didn't appreciate all the blessings he'd been granted.

Judging by Carli's expression, that's exactly what she was thinking.

Carli watched as Justin walked out of her office half an hour later, relieved to finally have some time to herself. What a strange morning it had been. It had taken all she had to remain cool and professional once he'd walked in here. She'd pulled it off, but barely. The whole while she was speaking with Justin regarding the business, her insides had felt like jelly. Thank heavens she hadn't eaten anything this morning. It probably wouldn't have stayed down.

The problem was, she wasn't sure what was causing all the turmoil. Sure, it had been upsetting when he'd so casually dismissed her as she was trying to introduce herself. And she'd known he was judging her by her appearance. But none of that was anything new for her.

People always underestimated her at first. She just made sure to prove herself, had been doing so her whole life. Not to mention, she'd had to find ways to somehow differentiate herself from her four siblings. Right smack in the middle, she was oh-so-easy to overlook. Tammy was the wise oldest sister, happily married with a lovely little boy. Janie, the beautiful one. People in their town actually called her JB, short for Janie Beautiful. Janie had the sort of looks that made men stammer when they spoke to her. While Carli was curvy and voluptuous, her next older sister was gorgeous in an angelic and soft way that Carli could never compete with. She certainly hadn't been able to last year...

Don't even start with that.

And the twins...well, they were twins. That fact alone made them stand out.

Carli was just the middle sister. Nothing special there. Barely noticeable in the crowd. So she made sure to work harder than any of them. Years of study and long hours, first at business school and then at the office, she hadn't taken anything for granted.

And now the arrival of the other Hammond son might be threatening all of that. No wonder she felt so out of sorts when Justin was near. She had to do something to fix that, but what exactly?

Jocelyn tapped lightly on her door before she could answer her own question.

"Come in."

"Hey, how did it go? Were you even able to focus?"

Carli shrugged as she opened her email inbox. "Of course," she said, though it was a fib. "Why in the world wouldn't I?"

"I'm sure I wouldn't have been able to. Not with those deep dreamy eyes focused on me."

Carli resisted the urge to grunt. "Not this again." No way was she going to admit, not even to herself, that there might be a kernel of truth to Jocelyn's words, that in fact it *had* been pretty distracting every time she'd looked up and found herself under the intense focus of Justin's gaze.

"Jocelyn, you need a date."

Her assistant groaned with frustration. "Don't I know it."

"Are you bringing anyone to the party tonight?"

She answered with a sad shake of her head. "I'm really looking forward to it, still. You're very sweet to host one every year."

Being sweet really had nothing to do with it. Carli loved throwing that regular yearly party. She'd been planning and shopping for it since October.

"Well, in any case, you need to stop focusing on Justin Hammond's looks or his appeal," she admonished the younger woman, though part of her was addressing herself. "For all intents and purposes, the man is our boss."

Jocelyn pulled out the chair across from Carli's desk and plopped into it. "I know, I know. I'm just admiring him from afar. I wouldn't dream of going after the man who owns part of the company I work for."

"Good, I'm glad to hear it."

A mischievous smile formed on Jocelyn's lips. "Besides, he hardly glanced in my direction when he was here. He was much more focused on someone else."

Carli didn't like where she was going with this. "I want no part in where you're trying to take this conversation."

Jocelyn leaned forward in the chair, gave her a smile that could only be described as wicked. "Oh, come on! You had to notice."

"Notice what?"

"The way he was looking at you. Or more accurately, how he couldn't look away."

"All I noticed was how to make sure I gave him all the information he needed to get himself situated. He just needed more info about how the company operates."

Jocelyn looked skeptical. "Right. Just admit it."

"I don't see the point." The last thing she wanted to talk about, in her office no less, was the way men looked at her. The way Justin had looked at her. Recalling the way his eyes had roamed over her sent a shiver down her spine even now.

"Does there have to be a point to everything?"

Carli couldn't help but smile. Had she ever been that lighthearted? She couldn't remember a time. Not even as a child. There was always too much to do. Always a mess to clean up or a sibling to look after.

"I'd just like to figure out why he's really here. After all these years," she said, trying to change the subject back to business.

Jocelyn shrugged slightly. "I thought it was just because James is going to be away for a while.

And that Mr. Hammond, as both their father and CEO, decided it would be a good time to bring him on board with his older brother otherwise occupied."

Carli knew that's how things looked on the surface. But it still didn't explain Justin's sudden appearance. She was more than capable of holding down the fort while James Hammond was away. That wasn't self-aggrandizing or conceit. The eldest Mr. Hammond had expressed the notion in countless ways over the years.

"I'm glad he is here!" Jocelyn exclaimed. "Things were getting way too droll around this place. We needed some excitement."

"You just like looking at him."

"No doubt!" Jocelyn actually giggled. "I mean, what's not to like? He's downright dreamy. I've been watching him for years in all the tabloids. With one exotic model after another. Or that actress, what's her name. She was in that romantic comedy last year. I hear he's single now though."

"Uh-huh."

"Personally, I'm of the opinion that he should try to find someone with more substance. I mean, what are the chances he would ever fall for an everyday, average woman though, right? Men like that never do. He's way too glamourous and worldly for that. Wouldn't you agree?"

Carli's request to finally terminate this conversation died on her lips when she noticed someone had arrived at her open door. The blood left her brain when she realized who it was. Justin.

How long had he been standing there? And how much had he heard?

If the floorboards opened up and swallowed her whole, it wouldn't be enough to lessen her mortification.

This was just fabulous. On top of everything else, now he was going to see her as nothing but an office gossip.

His reputation preceded him yet again, Justin thought as he hesitated outside Carli's office door. He'd caught just enough of the women's conversation to realize it was absolutely about him. Also that it was mostly one-sided. Carli had barely spoken a word. In fact, she appeared ready to give her assistant a hard shake.

The other woman's back was turned to where he stood, but Carli had clearly seen him.

Damn.

This was awkward. Unable to come up with anything appropriate to say, he simply cleared his throat. Jocelyn, the assistant, actually jumped in her chair.

Carli didn't take her disapproving eyes off her when she spoke. "Justin, something else I can do for you? Jocelyn was just leaving."

"Yes, yes, I was." Jocelyn bolted up and ran out of the room, making sure not to look Justin in the eye.

Carli motioned to the newly abandoned chair in front of her desk. "Please, have a seat." She glanced at her watch. "Though we don't have a lot of time before the staff meeting."

Her cheeks were flushed, and she wouldn't meet his eyes either. Still awkward.

"It's okay," he began, then sat. "This won't take long."

"What can I do for you?"

Justin swore under his breath. This was going to be even more uncomfortable after he'd walked in on the previous conversation. But it was too late to back out now. Besides, he owed her an apology. He took a deep breath. "Listen, I know we got off on the wrong foot. I mean this morning. At my father's house."

She quirked an eyebrow in surprise.

"I'm not usually so…"

"Rude?" she supplied as he trailed off.

"That's probably an accurate description. In my defense, I'd been traveling all night. Not that it's any kind of excuse."

"I agree. It's not any kind of excuse."

Wow. She was a tough one. He didn't need this; he was only trying to apologize. Albeit doing a terrible job at it. But instead of being annoyed by her directness, he found it somewhat intriguing. Refreshing in a way. Most people didn't bother to challenge him under any circumstances. Carli Tynan was clearly not like most people. Her gaze pinned him where he sat. He hadn't noticed before just how her eyes appeared to go from deep chocolate to hazel when the light hit her face a certain way. Or the fullness of her lips, even as tightly pursed as they were at the moment.

"You're right. I just wasn't expecting to see anyone in my father's house that early. Especially someone like you, coming down the stairs at that hour. My mistake."

Her eyes grew wide, and the color in her cheeks heightened to a deep shade of red. Her grip on the pen she held grew so tight that her knuckles turned pale. This did not bode well, he thought.

"What are you saying exactly, Mr. Hammond?" she asked through gritted teeth. Uh-oh. He'd just gone from being Justin to Mr. Hammond in the span of a few moments.

"Nothing. I mean, I'm simply trying to clear the air. To explain my reaction upon seeing you."

"Maybe you should do that. Explain exactly what your reaction was when you first saw me this morning."

She threw it out like a challenge. One he wasn't foolish enough to even attempt to accept. He'd begun this apology all wrong. But the conversation he'd overheard between Carli and her assistant had thrown him off. Heck, Carli herself kept throwing him off. It was like he didn't even know how to behave around her.

Where was it coming from?

"Never mind. It's not important," he said, hoping she would drop the whole matter.

Apparently, that was too much to hope for. He should have known better. She immediately shook her head. "No, please clarify. I'm very interested in what exactly it is you're trying to say."

The woman was relentless. "Look, it's not important. I simply wanted to offer an apology."

She studied him in a way that made him feel like a lab specimen under a microscope. Perhaps some sort of insect. If he wasn't so damn uncomfortable, he would have almost laughed at her scorn at him.

"Which you still haven't done," she said.

"What?"

"I've yet to hear an apology. Or a valid explanation, for that matter."

His mouth grew dry. Damn it, he was a successful executive, known for his cut-throat business style and ruthless negotiation skills. How was this woman cutting him off at the knees? And why was he almost enjoying it?

"Um? Explanation?"

She gave him a smirk of a smile, like he'd been caught. He supposed he had. "For why you behaved as you did. I was simply delivering a file at your father's request. And instead of introducing yourself, you dismissed me and practically shooed me out of the house."

Justin cringed at her description. He couldn't believe he'd been such a boor to her. Nor could he believe the way he was botching this apology now. Not only had be managed to insult a valuable Hammond employee, he couldn't even apologize for it in a sufficient manner. True to form, when it came to anything Hammond related, Justin was woefully lacking. He may have started his own wildly successful consulting firm and grown it from a one-man operation to a major international business. But when it came to being a Hammond, all he'd ever managed was failure. More proof that he didn't belong here back in Boston. Or at Hammond's Toys for that matter.

He had to pull himself together. Find a way to explain himself. But how? It's not like he could come out and admit to jumping to the worst conclusion—suspecting Carli to be his father's mistress. Though it was obvious she'd figured it out. If looks could kill and all that.

Nothing to do now but be completely straight. And hope the damage could be repaired somehow. He and Carli would be working together for the next several days. She was clearly a major asset to this corporation, and he had managed to insult her in a major way. He had to fix this.

"The truth is there is no excuse or explanation for the way I behaved. Please believe that it had nothing to do with you personally and everything to do with my father."

She remained silent, not ready to give an inch.

"I can only say I'm sorry," he added. "And that I will somehow find a way to make it up to you."

She shrugged with derision, and though she didn't say the words, her response was clear: *as if you could.*

Maybe she was being petty, but Carli wasn't going to give him the benefit of a response. Justin Hammond had made a horribly insulting assumption about her and the older man she worked for. That's something she would not readily forget.

Still, she couldn't help but feel more than a little touched at his genuine apology. Even given how badly he'd botched it up. He really did seem to feel remorseful. If the circumstances were different, if he weren't the boss's son and instead they were somehow new friends, she might have explained to him that she'd been dealing with such impressions all her life.

But he *was* a Hammond. And they definitely were not friends.

She would do her best to help him while he was here and hope that his tenure at Hammond's Toys was a short one. The events of this morning proved that Justin was walking in blind. He'd had no clue who she was or just how much she was in charge of. She didn't have time to babysit the prodigal son on a long-term basis.

She stood up from her chair and walked around her desk. "Well, I guess the prudent thing to do would be to move on and try our best to work together as productively as possible."

Justin stood, as well. He looked notably relieved. "I agree. And I appreciate it."

"We can start with this staff meeting. I asked Jocelyn earlier to forward you a copy of the agenda."

He nodded. "I got that. Thanks."

He followed her down the corridor to the meeting room where several employees had already gathered. After a brief round of introductions,

Carli began the meeting with the first item on the agenda.

The first time she stammered, she chalked it up to feeling exhausted and due to the mishaps of the morning. By the third mistake, however, she had to admit that she was off her game. She also had to admit that it had everything to do with the new face sitting at the table.

Justin leaned forward, listening attentively and frequently jotting down note after note. He preferred old-fashioned paper and pen, which surprised her. Most of the executives she dealt with couldn't wait to purchase and show off the latest technology e-tablet or the sleekest new laptop.

Aside from an occasional question or request for clarification, he was mostly quiet. Still, his presence was jarring.

She wasn't the only one who seemed to think so. Several furtive glances were cast in Justin's direction. One of the younger new recruits from sales smiled at him demurely, not even pretending to pay attention to Carli's updates. Though annoyed, she could hardly blame the other women. Justin had a presence. Add to that the mystery surrounding his arrival, and people were having trouble feigning indifference.

Herself included.

At the conclusion of the meeting an hour later, she was more than ready to be done and to get out of there. A cup of coffee would be heaven right about now. She hadn't been able to get her usual cup due to her detour, and a dull ache was beginning to throb behind her eyes. No doubt the caffeine withdrawal had been at least partly responsible for her less than stellar performance.

"Well, if that's everything, I think we can wrap up."

Everyone stood except for a few stragglers who stuck around to discuss their next to-do or to make small talk. Eventually, even they slowly filed out of the room.

In fact, when she looked up, Carli found that everyone had left except for one lone holdout. Justin remained seated. He studied her with avid interest. He clearly had something to say.

Carli set her jaw. Looked like her caffeine hit was going to have to wait. "Was there something else, Justin?"

"Yes, as a matter of fact. If you have a few moments, I think there are some things we should probably discuss. Sooner rather than later."

Something in his tone made her stomach twist. She sat back down.

"Go on."

"I've been going over the numbers, and Hammond's profit margins are mostly impressive. But there are areas that are lagging."

"I'm aware of that."

"Then you also realize that a handful of the retail stores have seen steadily declining sales."

"I'm aware of that too. There are several ideas in the pipeline to address this. As I just mentioned."

He glanced down at the notes in his leather-bound notebook. "Yes, I heard. All well-thought-out ideas involving online expansion. The modifications to the website are particularly impressive."

"But?"

"My concern is that there's a need to remove some of the more sluggish units, so to speak. Hammond's should be making some cuts."

"What sort of cuts?" she asked, though she

knew exactly where this was headed. The twist in her stomach turned a bit tighter.

"With your background and experience, I'm sure you've concluded which brick-and-mortar stores are just not pulling their weight. In fact, their only real profits register during the holidays."

"It's a very seasonal business."

"Nevertheless. Some of these stores just don't get enough foot traffic during the year to justify keeping them open." He glanced down at the file she had handed him just hours ago. "There's one in particular we need to seriously consider the future of. It hasn't seen any kind of significant sales for the past half decade."

Carli bit down on her lip. She knew exactly which store he was referring to. The one she'd started out in as a lowly retail clerk trying to save enough money for college. The same store that currently employed several people she'd grown up knowing and caring for. The one situated at the heart of Westerson, MA—a quaint, touristy spot along the inland coast of Cape Cod in Massachusetts. The same town she'd grown up in.

And Justin wanted to shut it down.

CHAPTER THREE

HER PARTY GUESTS were going to be here within the hour, and Carli was just now stepping out of the shower. So far, this day had been nothing but one big race against the clock. She should have started prepping as soon as she got home. Instead, she'd taken the time to go over the sales figures.

Not that there was any use, and Carli had known it. But she'd hoped for some small miracle that had somehow been missed. Something, anything she could use as leverage to argue that Justin should nix the idea of closing the doors of the Cape store for good.

Of all the retail stores in the Hammond chain, why did that have to be the one performing the worst? She'd practically grown up in that store. Mr. Freider, the manager going on twenty years, had always welcomed her with open arms. As a child, she'd go into that store by herself, just to pass the time in peace when things were just too noisy at home. During her teenage years, she'd spent countless hours in the Book Nook, the corner of the store dedicated to latest in children's and young adult books. She'd devoured a world of stories in that small area, Mr. Freider never complaining about her lack of purchases—purchases she couldn't afford. In fact, he'd been kind enough to bring hot chocolate on cold days and sweet lemon iced tea during summer.

That same kind man would very well lose his job if it were up to Justin.

There had to be something she could do. Perhaps she could go straight to Jackson. Plead her case. The only problem was, she didn't really have a professionally sound one. Essentially, that would amount to asking for a favor, as his protégé. As steep as the stakes were, she couldn't bring herself to do that. She'd never once approached Jackson Hammond as anything less than a professional and wouldn't start now. Not even under these circumstances.

Carli blinked away the thoughts. She had to get going already; no doubt some of the invitees would be straggling in early, ready to party on this cold December Boston evening without much else to do. She hadn't even towel dried her hair yet.

What had possessed her to plan a Christmas party on a Wednesday night anyway? And just her luck, it had happened to fall on the same day that Justin Hammond had blown into town and thrown her whole world into a spiral.

Now she was running late and dripping wet just as most of her colleagues were about to descend on her apartment for some yuletide Christmas cheer. A timer went off in the kitchen, a reminder to take the crab cakes out of the oven. Thank goodness she'd put out all the decorations weeks ago, the day after Thanksgiving. A tradition from her childhood. Exactly as Justin had guessed. The Tynan family may not have had much in the way of material things, but they made sure to celebrate their ceremonial traditions. Ceremonies that often got downright unruly and chaotic. She supposed that was to be expected in a family of five children.

By some Christmas miracle, she was ready when the first guests arrived: Jocelyn and some of the account reps along with a couple of regional managers. Carli didn't even recognize two of the arrivals. That's what happened when you posted an open invite. She didn't mind. These people were her second family now, Hammond's Toys was her second home. She was lucky to have such an opportunity with such a wonderful company. Current situation with the boss's son notwithstanding.

In fact, an hour later when the party was in full swing and several champagne bottles had been corked, she found herself blessedly distracted and finally able to enjoy herself. Until one of the elderly secretaries walked in. She wasn't alone.

"I hope you don't mind," Miranda Sumpter said, her gray hair framing her maternal face. "I brought someone with me."

Carli tried to hide her surprise. Justin, to his credit, looked less than pleased to be there.

Miranda was staring at her expectedly. "I mean, it said open invitation on the company wide email. And Justin's definitely part of the company. You don't mind, do you?"

"Yes! No! I mean. Of course he's welcome." Now Justin just looked bemused. Carli gripped her glass flute in her hand tight enough that her fingers ached. Then she took a large swig.

Justin stepped toward her. "I didn't realize you'd be the host, Carli."

Well, how was she supposed to respond to that? Was the implication that he wouldn't have come if he'd known?

Miranda stood staring at the two of them as an awkward silence settled. Carli cleared her throat. "So, how do you two know each other?" she finally managed to ask.

Miranda gave Justin's arm an affectionate squeeze. "Oh, he and I go way back. I used to babysit this little hurricane when he was no more than a mischievous toddler. When I first started out in the Hammond secretarial pool and needed some extra cash."

She turned to Carli. "They were always looking for a sitter for this one. Couldn't handle him without a little help. He was constantly getting into trouble."

He still was, Carli thought. If the tabloids were to be believed.

"I just about fell over when I saw him in the

hallway this afternoon," Miranda continued. "Almost didn't recognize him."

Justin gave her a playful wink. "I've changed just a bit, huh?"

"You still look plenty mischievous." The older woman laughed. "You should have seen some of the disasters he used to get himself into," Miranda said Carli. "Always in trouble. His parents were at their wits' end most days."

The tone was lighthearted, Miranda laughing merrily. But Carli couldn't help but notice Justin fidgeted as she spoke. He turned the watch on his wrist and pulled on the band. He was clearly uncomfortable. Probably regretted having come here now that he realized this was her party.

"I've since matured a bit," he offered.

"I would certainly hope so." Miranda laughed again. "You were quite the hellion."

"Yes, I recall my parents not being able to wait to rush out of the house as soon as you showed up."

Carli detected an undercurrent in his tone, a hardness. As the middle daughter in a family with five girls, she could certainly relate to growing up in a chaotic, messy household. But she couldn't remember her parents ever trying to "rush out" to get away from any of them. Lord knew, they'd given both Mom and Dad plenty of reasons to want to.

"At least I got to leave at the end of the night. Your parents were stuck with you, weren't they?" Miranda gave him a playful pinch on the cheek.

"I'm surprised you kept coming back."

"There were plenty of times I was tempted not to."

For such a playful conversation, Carli couldn't help but feel slightly uncomfortable. All she really knew about the Hammonds was that the parents had split while the boys were ten and twelve respectively. And for some unfathomable reason, one parent stayed with one son while the other took off with the other to live on the West Coast. She knew for a fact James hadn't seen his mother more than once or twice since the divorce. And she suspected the same of Justin and his father.

It was an incredibly sad scenario if one really thought about it. For all the turmoil and hassles of growing up with four siblings, Carli couldn't imagine years going by without seeing any one of them. Even after what had happened last year between her and her sister Janie.

She winced at that memory before realizing that Justin had just said something to her. Also, Miranda had excused herself and walked away.

"I'm sorry, I missed what you said."

"I was commenting on how festive your apartment is. You've obviously put a lot of effort into decorating for the holidays."

It was clearly an attempt to change the subject, but she couldn't help but feel a little flattered at the compliment.

She was about to give him a warm smile and answer that this decorative effect had taken weeks to achieve. But then she remembered what he wanted to do with the Cape Cod store.

"Thank you," she said with a curt nod. "Now, if you'll excuse me, I have other guests I should attend to."

Justin watched Carli walk away and grabbed a glass of wine off one of the trays sitting in the corner. It was hard not to appreciate the view as she made her way across the room. The woman was shaped like sin.

Looked like his apology hadn't quite cut it as it was clear she was still unhappy with him. He wasn't sure why that bothered him so much. It really shouldn't have. He'd only just met the woman this morning. They wouldn't even be working together for that long. He'd do what was asked of him by his father and return to the West Coast in a few days. Really, the opinion of some midlevel executive at Hammond's Toys should be the last thing on his mind.

Still, he had to admit he was vexed. His transgression toward her this morning wasn't that bad. Was it?

He bit out a silent curse as he thought about it. Yeah, he was fooling himself. It was bad. To assume she was his father's mistress. Simply based on the hour of the day and the way she looked. He couldn't blame her for still being upset.

Doubtful his older brother, James, would have ever been careless enough to make such a mistake. No, James probably always displayed the utmost professionalism and leadership. Usually, Justin wouldn't hesitate to describe himself the same way. Apparently not when he was here, however. In Boston and around Hammond Enterprises, Justin was out of his element to the point of near incompetence.

Clearly, Justin was a Hammond in name only.

The question was, what was he going to do about it as far as Carli was concerned?

Someone tapped on his shoulder as he tried to find Carli from the crowd of people in her apartment. He turned to find a petite, dark-haired woman smiling at him. It took him a minute to recognize her. Jocelyn, Carli's assistant. She looked different without the professional ponytail she'd been wearing this morning.

"Well, hello," Jocelyn said, loud enough and with enough enthusiasm that two people turned to see who had spoken.

"Hello."

"I didn't expect to see you here."

He spread his arms and bowed slightly. "Here I am."

"Fantastic. We were sort of sad that James was going to miss it this year. And here you are in his place."

Justin tried not to snort with irony. As if there was any way he would ever be able to take his brother's place in any way, shape, or form. Not as far as Hammond's was concerned. And certainly not in his father's eyes.

He gave Jocelyn a neutral smile. "Glad I could make it."

"I'm glad Carli saw to it that you came," Jocelyn said, and took a sip of her ruby red wine.

He had no intention nor desire to correct her. Actually, he had no intention of staying around much longer. There was no feasible reason he hadn't left as soon as Carli walked away.

Other than some silly desire to see her again this evening. Funny how he'd never been a glutton for punishment until this very day. Carli didn't want anything to do with him.

He spotted her coming out of the kitchen with more drinks. Several people stopped her along the way; she gave one woman an affectionate air kiss. Several men approached her as well, one taking part of the load off her hands. They seemed friendly but not overly familiar. These men were all clearly just colleagues.

Not that it was any of his business. For all he knew she already had a steady boyfriend or partner. Women who looked like Carli and who had as much going for them weren't single for long.

Jocelyn waved a hand in front of his face. "Hello? Where'd you just drift off to?"

He smiled apologetically. "Sorry, I was just admiring all the Christmas decorations. Carli's got quite a talent for it."

"Really? Is that what you were admiring?"

Uh-oh. He had to be careful here. He couldn't be caught ogling his father's project manager. "What else?"

She gave him a knowing look but luckily dropped the matter. "Anyway, I'm glad two Hammond men will be at Carli's party after all."

Justin turned his full attention to her. "Excuse me?"

"You and your father. He never misses one of Carli's soirees."

Damn. The last thing Justin needed was to run into his father right now. Their brief meeting this morning had been awkward enough.

"I don't see him yet though," Jocelyn added. "He always seems to arrive much later. Likes to make an entrance."

That definitely sounded like the attention-craving father Justin remembered from his childhood. And from everything he'd been told or had read about the man.

He still had the chance to make his getaway before Jackson arrived. All the more reason to leave right now. So, what was stopping him?

He should have never come in the first place. He knew it had been a mistake. He never even went to these events at his own company. But seeing Miranda again after all these years, remembering how she'd always been so kind to him. Even as he'd been making her life miserable with one childish antic after another.

Still, he had every intention of gently turning Miranda down. But the woman had not taken no for an answer.

Someone turned up the volume on the sound system and "Holly Jolly Christmas" started pounding through the room. Great. Now he was going to have to put up with the damn Christmas carols again.

Jocelyn squealed as the song came on. He'd almost forgotten she was standing in front of him. Again. "I love this song!" she exclaimed. "Let's dance!"

Before he had a chance to protest, she pulled

him into the center of the room where two other couples were already bouncing along to the tune. This wasn't the traditional version of the song he was used to. It was a bouncy, bassy remake of some sort. With a bit of urban rap lyrics thrown in between verses. As if the original song wasn't annoying enough. He was supposed to dance to this?

Pretty much a version of hell. Still, he knew what to do. Several years of mandated dance lessons thanks to his society-norm-conscious mother came in handy during moments like this. He matched Jocelyn's steps and earned a girly giggle when he dipped her.

By the time the song ended, Jocelyn was smiling from ear to ear. "You are quite a dancer, Mr. Justin Hammond."

"I am a man of many talents."

"Well, I don't want to hog you all to myself," she said, and before he knew it, she had somehow managed to steer them toward where Carli stood talking to a middle-aged man with a bad comb-over.

"You are the host of this party. You should be dancing too," Jocelyn admonished as she pulled

Justin in front of her. "Justin is a terrific dancer. And he needs a partner." She turned to comb-over guy. "Tom, may I have the honor of this dance?"

Justin watched with both bemusement and dismay as Jocelyn and Tom walked onto the middle of the floor and started dancing.

"My assistant is not subtle," Carli said. "Obviously."

"Does that mean you're not interested in dancing with me?"

She tilted her head. "I'd never dream of making you dance. To a Christmas song, no less. I know how much you dislike them."

With that flippant comment, she tried to walk away. But he wasn't going to let her. It was about time they hashed out some stuff, he figured. Otherwise, he was just going to keep letting her get under his skin. That would not bode well for either of them. Even if he was only going to be around her for a few days.

"On the contrary, I'd love a dance," he said as he gently took her by the arm and led her to the makeshift dance floor.

The protest died on her lips as he spun her

around toward him and started swaying with her to the music. He was close enough to sniff a hint of her perfume, a flowery subtle scent. Jasmine perhaps. It suited her.

As did the cocktail dress she wore, a silky, drippy number that hung on her curves in a tasteful, flattering way. He noticed she had whimsical snowman earrings dangling from her dainty lobes.

"See, I can dance to anything. Even annoying versions of Christmas songs."

She gave an exasperated huff. "How can you not like Christmas carols? There's got to be one that you're fond of."

He shook his head. "Can't think of one."

"Not even 'Jingle Bells'?"

"I find that one particularly grating."

The look she gave him was one mixed with both sympathy and bewilderment.

Justin sighed. She must think him the biggest Scrooge. "Christmas wasn't quite the jolly and wonderful time in the Hammond household as it was for most people," he admitted.

He twirled her around playfully as he said it.

"Makes no sense, I know," he added. "Given

how we make our livelihood. In some ways it just made things worse."

"How so?"

"Well, for one thing, my father became even more obsessed with sales figures and profit projections. He'd go into the office early and come home late. Even more so than usual. His increased hours gave my parents yet one more excuse to argue."

He almost laughed at that. *Argue* was hardly an adequate word for the knockdown, soul-crushing fights his parents used to have.

"It made for less than a peaceful holiday," he added. Why was he telling her these things? This wasn't something he particularly liked to talk about with anyone. Let alone a woman he'd just met a few hours ago. A woman who'd made it painfully clear that she didn't seem to like him very much.

"That's so very sad. I can't imagine Christmas being a time of turmoil for a young child."

Well, now she felt sorry for him. "I wasn't looking for sympathy," he said, with a little more force in his voice than he'd intended. "Besides, it's not like I helped the situation. I was a bit of a frustrating child. As Miranda just pointed out."

"You were just a child."

"A rambunctious, unruly, very disobedient child."

She shook her head. "But still a child."

The look in her eyes was intense, he had the disquieting feeling she was looking deep into his soul in the most intimate way. What a silly notion that was. They were in the middle of an office holiday party, surrounded by people.

Before he could respond, the music changed. The upbeat, bouncy rhythm of "All I Want for Christmas" transitioned to the slow, rhythmic melody of "Baby, It's Cold Outside."

Carli immediately stopped. But he wasn't ready for this to end just yet. Whatever *this* was. Before he could give it too much thought and before she could turn to go, he stepped closer to her and took her by her waist. She felt warm and soft under the silky material of her dress. After a gentle nudge, she began to move with him to the slower tempo of the song.

Justin pulled her closer, until they were mere

inches apart. Her eyes grew wide with shock but she didn't make any kind of move to pull away.

Good thing, he thought. Because he wasn't sure he'd be able to let her go.

CHAPTER FOUR

WHAT IN THE world was she doing?

Carli knew she should excuse herself and slip out of Justin's arms. Instead, she just stayed there, lulling herself into the cocoon of his embrace. Not even the fact that her guests were starting to stare could seem to make her pull away. And they weren't merely guests, she reminded herself. These were her colleagues. She'd never been anything less than professional and straitlaced in front of every single one of them. But for the life of her, she couldn't bring herself to end the dance.

Justin was indeed an ideal dance partner. He moved with fluid grace and coordination. It was hard not to enjoy being with him this way.

More than that, she couldn't stop thinking about the things he'd just confessed to her about his childhood. She'd heard rumors about the Hammonds' failed marriage, of course. Hammond's Toys was no different than any other company when it came to office gossip. But she'd never given the matter much thought. And certainly neither James nor Jackson had ever broached the topic.

She'd had no idea things had been that bad before the marriage ended.

"Let's talk about something else," Justin said quietly in her ear. His proximity sent a shiver down her spine. "I'm bordering on party-pooper status here."

He'd just given her the perfect opportunity to bring up the disturbing topic that had been looming in her mind. The Cape Cod store. She could try to make a case for giving it another chance. The numbers weren't that bad, and surely they could be turned around. But she couldn't bring herself to answer with such a daunting subject. Not right now.

After all, was this really the time or place?

"What would you like to talk about?" she asked instead. She'd find some way to bring up the matter at some point. When the time was right.

And that decision had nothing to do with the way he was holding her right now.

"How about you? Tell me what your Christmases were like. You obviously have fonder memories related to the holiday than I do."

"What makes you say that?"

He laughed softly at the question. "It's rather obvious. One big clue is the sheer amount of decorations in here. You'd give the Hammond's Manhattan store a run for its money in comparison. The garland alone is impressively lavish."

"I have a confession to make," she admitted.

"What's that?"

"These are my regular Christmas decorations. Not just for the party."

His laughed once more, and Carli found herself smiling in return.

"This is what your place looks like under normal circumstances?"

"Only at Christmastime."

"And you did it all yourself?"

"Who else?"

He shrugged. "We always hired professional services to do our holiday decorating and to hang our lights. First at the house and then the various apartments my mom had us living in over the years."

Carli tried to imagine watching as strangers

handled her delicate ornaments, or the tiny figurines that made up her Christmas village. She treasured every one of those items. Some she'd paid for with her own hard-earned funds, and others had been cherished gifts from friends or relatives. Every piece was a part of her in a tiny yet significant way. Each time she set one out, it triggered a special memory. Some of them even made her homesick. The idea of strangers handling such sentimental trophies made her shudder.

It occurred to her that Justin had most likely never experienced anything like that.

"I can't imagine having someone else do it."

"And I can't imagine even knowing where to put anything."

She could show him, was her first thought. An unbidden image flashed in her mind of the two of them standing in front of a brick fireplace with a roaring fire as they hung stockings above the mantel. She blinked it away. How utterly ridiculous of her.

She really had to get a grip. This man was the boss's son. Which essentially made him her boss. There was a chance he was going to usurp her duties while he was here. And there was an even greater chance that he was going to shut down the store that had meant the world to her growing up. She had zero business dreaming up idyllic, romantic fantasies of the two of them.

And anyway, he was absolutely not her type. Not that she even knew what her type was anymore. Not after the fiasco with Warren and his utter betrayal. In fact, she decided then and there that she no longer had a type. She'd sworn off men entirely. At least until she was fully established in her career.

Justin was invoking sensations she'd held dormant for too long, and this was not the way she wanted to reawaken them. With a man who was so outrageously out of her league in every single way.

Blessedly, the song ended and she moved to step away from his embrace.

But a commotion of noise and boisterous cheers distracted them both before she could excuse herself.

Jackson Hammond had just arrived.

Justin knew the exact moment his father walked in. He didn't have to see Jackson to know he was here. Even if other guests hadn't been calling out Jackson's name in greeting, Justin would have sensed his presence. The air changed whenever someone like his father entered a room.

The magic of dancing with Carli seemed to dissipate as the real world returned along with his father's arrival. He sighed slowly and let her go. Served him right. He'd forgotten for a brief moment that he wasn't one of those men who could dance carefree with a beautiful woman in her quaint, charming apartment full of holiday cheer.

Damn it. He should have left when he'd had the chance. What had he been thinking? Allowing himself to be distracted by Carli and her notions of perfect Christmases with happy memories. Now he had to make nice with the father he'd barely seen in several years who for some sudden, inexplicable reason had needed his expert financial advice.

He wasn't even curious as to why. He honestly didn't care. He just wanted to do what was asked of him and return to his life. There was nothing in Boston that endeared it to him. Though he couldn't help but glance at Carli as that thought flitted through his head. If only he'd met her in a different time, under different circumstances.

And if only he'd been a completely different man.

"Looks like dear old Dad is here," he remarked.

Jackson made a beeline right to where they stood as soon as he spotted them. Smiling, he placed a firm grip on Justin's shoulder. "I didn't expect to see you here, son."

Justin winced inwardly at the last word. "Miranda can be quite persuasive."

"She always did have a soft spot for you." He turned to Carli and gave her a nod. "I see you've met the host of this lovely get-together. She's also better known as my right hand."

"Justin and I have gotten to know each other a bit over the past few hours," Carli offered.

If his father had any kind of untoward feelings for his young, beautiful project manager, he was doing an excellent job at hiding it. Maybe Jackson had indeed changed and was no longer the notorious philanderer his mother had frequently accused him of being. More likely, Carli was the type of professional who would not abide that type of attention from a man she worked for.

Justin hadn't known her for long, but he realized now what a huge error in judgment it had been to even entertain the notion that Carli would be the type of employee who would date her elderly boss.

"Yes, she's been very helpful. The report she prepared and delivered held a wealth of useful information. Enough that I was able to make some quick initial judgments."

Jackson studied him. Was that appreciation he detected in the old man's eyes? Probably more for his protégé and the file she'd prepared, Justin figured.

"Well, I don't like to get into business discussions at these events," Jackson said. "Let's go over everything tomorrow, the three of us, and you can tell me what you've concluded."

Justin was ready to agree when Carli surprised him by holding her hand up. "Wait. I'd like to say something about all this."

Both men turned to look at her. She appeared downright apprehensive. "Carli, do you have an issue with meeting tomorrow?" Jackson asked. "Is your schedule full?"

She shook her head, a tight firm line to her lips. "No, my schedule isn't the issue, Mr. Hammond."

"Then what is it?"

She turned to Justin. "I know what your first recommendation is going to be, Justin. And I'd urge you to reconsider."

"Reconsider?"

She swallowed. "Yes, I know you're going to argue that Hammond's should close the Cape store. And I realize you're the expert. But I think that would be a big mistake."

"I don't understand."

She inhaled on a deep breath. "If that's indeed your recommendation, I'm afraid I'll be fighting your decision."

Jackson at that point stepped slightly between them. "All right. Clearly we have some things to discuss. But I think we should save it for the office. This is not the time or place."

Carli looked ready to argue but then abruptly closed her mouth and looked away. "You're right, Mr. Hammond."

Justin nodded his agreement as an awkward silence descended. Finally, Justin excused himself and went to grab his coat hanging from the rack by the front door. He'd give his regrets to Miranda later about having left without saying goodbye. Right now, he had other things on his mind.

Looked like he and Carli Tynan were about to butt heads on yet another matter.

CHAPTER FIVE

SHE WAS EARLY; it had been impossible to sleep. Carli adjusted the collar of her business jacket and took a sip of her coffee. Jackson and Justin would be here in a few minutes. She was more than prepared to try to make her case, but the enormity of the task was not lost on her. The facts were definitely not on her side. How in the world was she supposed to convince a hard-nosed, by-the-numbers businessman that he should keep open a store that was seeing declining profits?

He'd appeared somewhat shocked last night at the party. She hadn't meant to blurt it out. But there was no way she could have kept quiet knowing where it was all leading.

Jackson's idea was that they sit together first thing this morning and hammer it all out.

Pulling out a chair at the long mahogany conference table, Carli took a deep breath and sat down. The whole floor was eerily quiet. No one else had come in yet. Traffic outside on Boylston Street had yet to pick up. The sun just now starting to burn through the crisp winter air.

The dinging of the elevator signaled the arrival of someone else. She glanced at her watch. Still another twenty minutes. So she was surprised when Justin appeared in the doorway. Dressed in a white shirt and silk navy tie, he looked every bit the successful tycoon.

Such a different image than the one he had projected last night at her party. Then he'd been casual, lighthearted. He'd danced with her, confided in her. He'd been friendly and open. Until the whole matter of the store.

He gave her a tight nod before entering the room. "Carli. Good morning."

"Justin."

"I see we're both early."

There was no hint of the genteel man who had swayed with her to hip-hop Christmas carols last night. The thought tugged at her heart. How she wished they could just sit down and discuss all this as just two friends who happened to work for the same company.

But Justin gave no indication that he was feeling at all friendly. The man was solidly in back-to-business mode. So be it. There was really only one objective here.

He glanced at his watch. They were both thinking the same thing: the sooner Jackson got here, the sooner they could get this all over with.

"There's coffee in the break room," she offered. For lack of anything else to say. The awkward silence was starting to rankle her.

"I've already had three cups this morning," he said dismissively.

"Oh."

"Thanks though," he said, his tone softer this time.

It was Carli's turn to check the time. She glanced at the classic wall clock behind Justin. Only five minutes had passed. What were the chances Jackson would be early for once in his life? Slim to none, she figured.

Clearing her throat, she made one more attempt at light conversation. "So, did you have fun last night? At the party?"

He looked up from his cell phone, his eyebrows lifted. "Yes, I was having a great time." At his words, she realized how much fun she'd been having too. The way Justin had held her, how warm his arms had felt around her waist as they danced.

"Even with all the annoying Christmas music playing?"

He smiled at her. "Yes, even so."

Her mind automatically recalled the way it had felt to slow dance in his arms. The hammering of her pulse at the way he'd held her, pulled her closer to him on the dance floor. She'd felt his heartbeat against her chest, and it had served to accelerate her own.

It had been months since she'd even been out on a date, let alone been touched by a man. And to have that man be Justin Hammond of all people. She'd been thinking about it all night, when she wasn't fretting about this meeting.

Like a silly girl with a crush.

"I'm glad you came last night," she admitted, surprising herself. "I probably should not have brought up the matter of the store. It was really not the time nor place."

He merely shrugged.

"You're probably not used to being second-guessed. And I understand why that would make you frustrated," she began, and then cringed as the words left her mouth. The phrase was straight out of a management training handbook or seminar on dealing with difficult colleagues. She could tell by his expression that the same thought had occurred to him.

Carli hated this. This wasn't her. She was usually the articulate, straightforward professional who knew exactly what to say to get her point across. With Justin she just seemed to keep stumbling.

"That's not quite the word I would use."

She was trying to come up with an answer to that when he suddenly stood. "Perhaps I will go get a cup of coffee," he said, and moved to the door. "Would you mind texting me when Jackson comes in?"

He left the room before she could say yes.

Justin paced the hallway outside the break room and felt his phone vibrate with Carli's text. He'd had no intention of getting any coffee; the last thing he needed was more caffeine. He'd just had to get out of that conference room.

Carli Tynan affected him like no other woman

he'd ever known. What had all that been about last night? He'd been about to give his father an overview of his observations on the retail operations when she'd cut him off like he was an errant child. Then she'd made some cryptic remark about how he was wrong on one major point, and she wanted a chance to explain.

Jackson had stepped in then and suggested they all meet this morning to get to the bottom of it all. Not that it would prove useful. Justin could guess what was happening. Carli must feel unsettled that he was here now. She'd been the one running the show alongside his brother and father. No doubt she felt threatened because of his presence.

He didn't even really blame her.

Well, now that his father was here, they could finally get to the bottom of it, once and for all.

He found Jackson at the head of the conference table when he arrived back in the meeting room. He nodded in greeting. Carli remained where she had been seated.

"Now, what's this all about, you two?" Jackson wasted no time.

Justin paused. Damned if he knew. He waited for Carli's answer.

She cleared her throat. "As you know, I prepared some figures and analysis for Justin like you requested."

"Thank you for getting that done so quickly," Jackson told her.

"You're welcome. It was just a matter of pulling together all the info."

"It was all very useful information," Justin added.

"So what's the problem, Carli?" his father asked.

She appeared visibly nervous. "I know Justin has come to some conclusions based on the information."

"That's correct," Justin jumped in. "Several issues can be addressed to increase profit margins. Some major, some minor."

"It's one of the more major ones that I have an issue with," Carli said. "Something Justin mentioned yesterday that he is considering."

Both men waited for her to continue.

"Justin is thinking of closing one of our stores. The one on the Cape. I have to stress that I think that would be a big mistake."

That's what this was all about? The closing of a store that was bleeding cash? If he recalled correctly, that particular location hadn't been in the red for about five years.

"I see," Jackson said, rubbing his chin.

Justin looked from one of them to the other. "I'm afraid I don't. The store is nothing but a drain. Frankly, I'm surprised no one's suggested shutting its doors before this."

"I'm very familiar with that store, Justin. I grew up in Westerson. Even worked there as a teen. It's how I ultimately came to work for Hammond's Toys corporate office. I'm personally aware of all it's potential."

Ah, so this was all about the human factor, even if Carli didn't want to admit it. Perhaps not even to herself. But as a businessman, every part of his being told him that something had to be done. The store just wasn't viable as a business unit.

"The fact of the matter is, that location cannot continue to run as a viable retail store. It's just not performing. That's my professional opinion."

Carli set down her pen. "But perhaps if we

could just give it a chance to turn things around. I know the head manager. He's very hardworking. And flexible. He's been ill the past few years. But now that he's back on his feet, I think he'll be able to make the store profitable again now that he can devote all his time."

"I don't see how," Justin countered.

"There are several ways. For one, logistically the bulk of the town's children are getting older, so we'll need to invest more in things like video games and high end technology toys like drone flyers. Like I said, the store manager just hasn't been able to spend as much time on following the trends. But he's fine now."

"And if he gets sick again?" Justin knew it sounded like a cold and heartless question. The way she sucked in her breath and shot a surprised look at him said she thought so too. Something shifted in his chest at the thought that he'd disappointed her. He squelched it down.

He felt for Carli. He really did. But he'd been asked his professional opinion. He would have to be honest giving it. "I was asked to come here and offer my analysis based on experience. And to make suggestions. I'm only stating the facts. The brick-and-mortar stores are not where the sales are. Their expenses continue to grow as their sales slide more and more every year. This particular store is probably just the start."

Jackson raised a hand; he'd been surprisingly silent up until now. "I believe there's really only one way to approach this," he began.

Carli and Justin both looked at him expectedly. When he spoke again, it was with clear authority. "I'm going to have both of you go to the Cape for a few days. Look at the store, make some observations. See if there are indeed any opportunities to turn things around."

Carli's jaw dropped. Justin was taken a bit aback himself. What was there to see at the physical location that the file hadn't already told him?

"But Mr. Hammond—" Carli began before Jackson stood and stopped her with a curt nod.

"That's my final say." He pushed his chair in. "I'd like you both to spend at least a week. This is the ideal time to go. Right before Christmas. Go to the Cape. Make the decision together. We'll regroup once you get back."

* * *

A whole week? This was a disaster in the making. How was she supposed to spend a whole week with Justin? In her hometown, no less?

Carli shut her office door and leaned back against it. She had to somehow get her mind around this new development. All she'd wanted to do was make a case this morning to give the Cape store some more time to turn things around. Not in her wildest imaginings would she have guessed this would be the result.

This was so not the way she'd imagined returning home after everything that had happened last year. The truth was, she wasn't even sure if she was ready to go back. It was all too fresh. Sure, her family had come to visit her in Boston, even Janie. But she hadn't been able to make her way back to town. Not yet.

Now she was going to have to do it with Justin Hammond in tow.

A knock on her door startled her. She opened it to find Justin on the other side.

"I suppose we better discuss some of the logistics," he said as she showed him in. She motioned for him to take a seat.

"We should probably leave within a day or so," she said with a sigh. "It's about a three-hour drive. Depending on traffic."

"I didn't bother to rent a car. I'll have to do that."

"Don't be ridiculous. I can drive you. It's my hometown." Not like she had a real choice. It would have been rude and unprofessional to not offer him a ride. Though no doubt it would be the longest ride of her life. "I'll pick you up from the house tomorrow morning."

"Can you recommend a place to stay?" he asked.

Carli nodded. "I'll have Jocelyn arrange it. There's a nice B and B near the beach. Within walking distance of the store."

"What about you?"

She shrugged. "I can stay with my parents. My childhood room is still empty, believe it or not."

"Won't that be a burden? On your mom and dad on such short notice?"

She blinked at him. A burden? On her own parents? The thought would never have occurred to her. Or her parents, for that matter. In fact, she was certain her parents would absolutely be thrilled that she was finally making her way back. "No. My parents are used to constant visitors at their house. I have a large family."

"How large?"

"I'm the middle child of five kids. All girls."

His eyes grew wide. "Wow."

"All my sisters still live in town. The younger ones are still in high school so still at home. My parents will hardly be fazed by another adult child visiting for a few days." They'd been gently pressuring her to do so for months. She didn't add that last part out loud.

He seemed to consider that like it was some sort of novel idea. Of course, he'd grown up with a single mom. Most likely in penthouses and palatial summer estates. Wait till he got a load of the small colonial house and rinky-dink town she'd grown up in.

"Maybe I'll get a chance to meet them all," Justin said, shocking her. She groaned inwardly. Introducing her worldly, sophisticated boss to the messy chaos that was her family was going to be another treat to this whole experience.

"I have no doubt," she told him. The Tynan clan wouldn't have it any other way. Once they found out she was in town with the other Hammond brother, all hell would break loose. Not just with her family either; the Westerson gossip mill would go into full swing.

"I'm sure my mom will want to feed you at some point. She's famous for her homemade lasagna."

He smiled at that. "That would be nice. I haven't had a home-cooked meal in I can't remember how long."

She couldn't tell if he was just being polite or if he really meant that. Probably the former, she decided. This man was used to dining in the finest restaurants all over the world, after all.

"Speaking of which, I should probably call her and let her know we're coming." She picked up her cell phone, already anticipating her mother's pleased excitement that she'd be returning after close to a year. Even if it was for business purposes.

Justin took the hint and stood to go. "Until tomorrow morning then."

CHAPTER SIX

By THE TIME Carli arrived to pick him up the next morning, Justin was ruing his decision to ever come back to Boston in the first place. He should have never listened to his mother. He should have put his foot down and told them both, her and his father, that he wanted nothing to do with Hammond's Toys. When all this was over, he was going to return to the West Coast and try never to set foot in this state again.

This trip to the Cape was futile. It wasn't going to warrant any more information. In the end, he would have to be firm and reiterate the decision he'd already made. And upset Carli further. His final opinion wasn't going to be any different; he would just have to break Carli's heart.

He refused to let himself feel guilty about that. This was simply business. She had to understand that. He would expect no less if the shoe were on the other foot.

How many times had he been turned down by venture capitalists when trying to launch various projects? He'd been immensely disappointed too every time it had happened. But he'd moved on, found another way.

The Westerson store and its employees could do the same. And besides, the final decision wasn't his. He was merely there as an outside consultant. He had no intention of fabricating an untruth simply to tell people what they wanted to hear.

He just hated that he'd be the one delivering the lesson.

That was a completely new experience for him. Never before had he second-guessed himself about delivering a recommendation. But now, for some inexplicable reason, he hated that he'd be the messenger of bad news. It had everything to do with Carli.

She pulled up in front of the driveway and popped her trunk open. After tossing his bag in, he slid into the passenger seat.

"Thanks for the ride."

"You're welcome. We should be there way before after noon sometime. I can take you to the inn, and then we can talk about where to start. Mr. Freider is expecting us."

Justin recalled the name as the store's manager. "Sounds good."

"And I hope you haven't made any plans for dinner," she told him.

He laughed to himself. What kind of plans would he possibly have? He didn't know a single person in the town he was about to visit. He barely knew a soul in all of New England. Except for Carli.

"None whatsoever. Why?"

"I was right about my mom. She insists we have dinner with them this evening. Won't take no for an answer."

"That's very nice of her."

She signaled and looked over her shoulder as they merged onto the highway. A double-wide semi blew past them, barely slowing down. He'd only been here a few days and had already found Boston drivers deserved their nasty reputation.

"You may not think so once you get there," Carli warned. He couldn't even tell if she was serious.

"Come again?"

"It won't be a quiet affair. Dinner at my parents' house never is. All four of my sisters will be there. One of them with her husband. Along with my nephew. Who may actually bring a friend."

Justin pulled down the visor against the harsh morning glare. How many people were going to be at this dinner? "That does sound rather, um, busy."

"You mean chaotic, don't you?" Carli asked, not taking her eyes off the road. "Like I said, they don't take no for an answer. I tend to pick my battles when it comes to my parents."

The way she said the last few words held a wealth of emotion. He had to wonder what the story was there. Then he had to wonder what made him so damn curious about this woman. It was really none of his business why her voice grew wistful sometimes as it had just now. Just like it had the last time she'd spoken of her family.

"Sounds like you're all very close." That much at least was clear.

"Sometimes I think we may all be way too close."

He waited for her to elaborate, but she didn't

expand on the comment. This was going to be a very long ride if he couldn't figure out a way to move the conversation forward. The last thing he wanted to do was bring up the closing of the store. That would just make the air too thick with tension. And how was he supposed to say anything relatable to her about her large family? He had only one sibling, and he'd rarely seen James over the years.

"You mentioned you have a young nephew?"

The tight line of her lips spread into a wide grin. "Yes, he's four. Quite a little dynamo." Her voice held genuine affection. Even a hint of awe.

"I have zero experience with children."

She gave him a quick side-eye. "Yeah, you don't really strike me as the babysitting type."

He chuckled. "Believe me, I'm not. I can't even keep a cactus plant alive."

"Well, don't let little Ray be a nuisance. He can be quite chatty. Just tell him to run along if he starts to bother you at dinner."

"How bad of a nuisance can he be?"

Carli's laugh was so deep and so sharp that he twisted in his seat to face her. "What?"

"You really haven't been around children, have you? And definitely not around four-year-olds."

"Never," he admitted.

"Well, you are in for a novel experience."

"I'm guessing you don't mean that in a good way?"

Her answer was another laugh.

"I'm starting to worry a bit," he admitted, only partially joking.

"Don't get me wrong. My nephew, Ray, is absolutely a little love. One of the biggest joys in my life. But he can resemble a tiny destructive tornado at times." She adjusted the heat setting on the dashboard, then continued, "It takes his two parents, all his aunties, a set of grandparents and practically most of the town to handle him. We take turns finding ways to channel all his considerable energy."

"It takes a village?"

"For Ray it certainly does." Despite her words, the love and affection she felt for her nephew were clear in the tone of her voice and the set of her jaw as she spoke about him.

Justin couldn't help but summon his own childhood memories. Carli was describing her nephew the same way he might have been characterized as a child. All he'd had were his mom and dad and slightly older brother. James was just a child, barely older than him. His father was gone most of the day. Various nannies and babysitters eventually just threw their hands up in utter defeat.

His mother was too busy trying to defeat her own demons to pay him any mind. The isolation had only grown worse when she'd finally left Jackson and James, taking only her younger son with her. They'd moved from one city to another, and she'd dated a string of men, never finding one who quite fit her needs.

His only paternal figures had been nannies who changed every time they moved. By the time he was a middle schooler, he'd known better than to develop any kind of affection for any of them.

Unlike Carli's nephew, Justin hadn't had anything resembling a village in his corner.

They were making good time until about halfway through the ride. Traffic suddenly slowed and then, much to Carli's dismay, became an annoying pattern of stop and go.

"Is there some sort of accident?" Justin asked.

Carli sighed and shook her head. "No. I'm afraid it's just impossible to time Cape traffic. You never know if you're going to hit a bottleneck."

"Sounds like California traffic," Justin commented.

"It's especially tricky this time of year, with the outlet mall along the way. Christmas shoppers looking for bargains."

"Another mark against the season."

Carli turned to look at him. How could he be such a downright Grinch? She gave her head an exasperated shake.

"What?"

"Nothing," Carli uttered as a mini-hatchback swerved and cut her off. "It's just that the irony of it all is almost too much. The second heir of Hammond's Toys, the biggest toy retailer in the Northern Hemisphere wants nothing to do with Christmas."

"Well, like I said at your party, we didn't celebrate like normal people. For us, it was mostly about the business. And things always got even more heated between my parents."

Carli felt a deep surge of sadness at his statement. He really had no clue what he'd missed out on. Or maybe he did. She couldn't decide which would be sadder.

"You don't have any good memories of that time of year? Not at all?"

"Not many." He seemed to hesitate. "There was maybe a…"

"What?"

"Nothing really. Just one time when I was about six. We were driving back from some store event, it was early evening. There was this drive-around with multiple light displays. The sign said Christmas Wonderland. I don't even remember what town it was."

He looked out the passenger side window. "Much to James's and my surprise, my father actually had the chauffeur drive through it. The displays and lights were magical. I thought so as a child anyway."

Carli felt a smile touch her lips. So he *was* human.

But then he added, "It was the first and last time we ever did anything like that."

How incredibly sad that as a child he hadn't

been exposed to more such experiences during the holidays.

Then she realized what was up ahead, just off the next exit. It was almost too perfect. And since they were just sitting here stuck in traffic anyway.

"You happen to be in luck," she told him.

"Yeah? How so?"

"We happen to be very close to just such a setup. It's not exactly a wonderland, so to speak. Just a town park to walk through. But every year they put up various Christmas displays and panoramas. Of course the lights won't be on this time of day, but we can go check out the decorations and everything else. I think we should stop in."

He laughed at the suggestion before turning to study her. "You're serious."

"Of course, I'm serious. It's just off the next exit. We can spend the time there waiting for the road to clear rather than sitting in stop-and-go traffic for an hour. It's not exactly as spectacular during the day, but it's better than watching rear taillights."

"Carli. It's really not necessary. It was just a

useless childhood memory in answer to your question."

Useless. Why was he so stubborn? Did he ever allow himself to do anything just for fun or kicks? "Then do it for me. I could use the time to stretch my legs on a little walk. Not to mention, they have a stand that serves the tastiest hot spiced cider. And I'm feeling a little thirsty."

He sighed in defeat. "Then far be it from me to keep you from quenching your sudden thirst. Or depriving you of a good leg stretch."

"Thank you. It's the least you can do for your long-suffering driver."

"My empathy knows no bounds."

That made her laugh, and she was still chuckling several moments later as she turned her blinker on and got off the expressway at the next exit. Moments later they pulled into the parking lot of the town recreation area, which was now set up as a holiday bazaar. A large sign at the gate read Santa's Village in big bright letters. Several children ran past it shrieking and laughing as three harried moms followed close behind.

"This is it," she declared as they both got out of the car.

"Why exactly are we doing this again?" Justin asked. Judging by the hint of a smile on his face, he couldn't be too put out about it.

She ignored the question. "Let's start with the cider."

"Whatever you say."

"Follow me."

He did so but paused as they approached the barn where several children were feeding the livestock. "Are those reindeer?" His disbelief was audible.

"They are indeed."

She took him by the arm and continued their walk. "I don't recommend petting them before we get the cider."

"I had no intention of petting them at all."

In her haste and distraction, Carli didn't notice the patch of ice before planting her foot square in the center. Her leg slid out from under her, and then the other leg followed and gave way. Carli braced herself for the fall and prepared for the impact of falling hard on her bottom.

Until a strong arm suddenly grabbed her by the waist and pulled her up. Instead of on the ground, she found herself braced against Justin's hard length. Her heart did a jump in her chest.

"Nice reflexes." Her voice caught as she said it. There was that spicy, sandalwood scent again. She fought the urge to lean in closer to get a better whiff.

"Careful," Justin admonished. "I'd hate to present you to your family with any broken bones." He made no attempt to let her go, and heaven help her she didn't try at all to pull away. Her gaze dropped to his chin. He'd nipped himself slightly with the razor, the smallest of cuts near his ear. That observation led to an unbidden image of him shaving in the morning, shirtless.

Carli sucked in a breath and tried to regain some focus. What had he just said? Oh, yeah, something about her breaking a bone. "Thank you for saving me from such a terrible fate. That would certainly put a damper on the holidays."

He smiled at her, and she had to remind herself to breathe. Reluctantly, she pulled herself out of his grasp. "For that, the cider is on me." On wobbly legs, she resumed walking, making sure to watch where she was going this time. She didn't need Justin to have to catch her in his arms a second time. Though it was more tempting than she wanted to admit.

That thought made her visibly shudder.

Justin must have misread her reaction as a response to the temperature. He removed his scarf and held it out to her. "Here. You appear to be cold."

She wasn't about to explain what her shiver had really been about. "I can't take your scarf."

He ignored that and stopped her with a hand on her arm. "The only reason you're out here in the cold is because I foolishly revealed some long-lost memory that you're kind enough to help me try to relive. The least I can do is give you my scarf." Turning her to him, he wrapped the featherlight material around her neck.

It smelled of him. Carli sank into the sensation of the soft material against her skin as this time she allowed herself to breathe in Justin's scent.

Carli cast a furtive glance in his direction as they continued walking. Once again, she had to remind herself he was her boss. And there was way too much at stake for her to entertain any romantic illusions where he was concerned. Regardless of how handsome she found him. The last thing she needed at this point in her career was any gossip that she'd gotten ahead professionally by pursuing the boss's second son. She'd had enough of gossip to last her an entire lifetime after her last relationship. According to her oldest sister, the hometown folks were still talking about the details of her breakup a year later. Even if most of it was concern on her behalf, it wasn't the kind of attention she needed nor wanted. Something like that would be all the worse if it was happening to her in a professional capacity.

Not to mention, she had no intention of getting her heart broken again. The wounds were still too fresh. Justin had just told her to be careful. He had no idea how hard she was trying. But it was becoming more and more tempting to throw caution to the wind with each passing moment she spent in his company.

The scent of spice and cinnamon grew stronger the farther they walked. Along the way, they passed display after display of Christmas scenes with moving figurines and colorful backgrounds. Justin found himself actually laughing at some of the funnier ones—including one of a large mechanical dog scarfing down the plate of cookies that had been left out for Santa.

Finally, they approached a small shed with a small line in front. The spot was without a doubt where the delicious aroma had been coming from.

Carli ordered for both of them and handed him a steaming hot cup.

"Be careful," she warned him just as he took it from her. "It's even hotter than it looks."

She waited with expectation as he took a sip. "Well?" she asked. "Was it worth the stop?"

It was good. But Justin didn't say what he was thinking. He didn't tell her that the stop had been worth it simply because of the way she'd looked at him earlier when he'd caught her before she fell. And for the way her bright chocolate eyes were studying him with anticipation right at this moment, simply to gauge his reaction to tasting the cider.

Instead of trying to find the words, he lifted the cup toward his temple in a mock salute.

Carli gave a whoop. "I knew you'd like it!"

The enthusiasm this woman displayed, the sheer enjoyment of the simple pleasantries around her was an utterly new experience for him. She definitely worked hard; what he'd witnessed back in Boston and the level of her success left zero doubt about that. But clearly also appreciated the blessing she'd been given in life. To witness it was like a magnetic pull for someone like him.

Outside of his employees or clients, when had anyone ever really cared what his opinion was? Or if he was enjoying something as simple as a glass of juice outside on a cold December day?

When had anyone bothered to do anything like try to find a way for him to relive a silly childhood memory?

"It's like drinking an apple pie," he told her.

"That's exactly the way it is." She looked around at the various displays surrounding them. "We used to come here every year when we were young children. We don't so much anymore. But it used to be tradition."

He took another sip of his cider and studied her over the rim of the foam cup. "You and your family seem to have had a lot of those."

"Doesn't everyone?"

He shrugged. "I guess I wouldn't know. We

didn't really. Unless you count lots of yelling and broken glass."

She reached out and placed a gentle hand on his arm. "You'll just have to start new ones then."

He hmmphed out an ironic laugh. Like what? All he ever wanted to do every Christmas Eve was watch an old baseball game on the DVR and enjoy a peaceful dinner alone. That was traditional enough for him. A picture popped into his head of someone with a startling resemblance to Carli Tynan sitting there at the table with him. He promptly shoved it out of his mind.

"What? It's never too late," she said softly next to him.

Justin didn't reply, just downed the rest of his beverage then tossed the cup into the trash can behind him. Carli hesitated for a moment before turning around. "Come on. Let's go say hello to Santa."

Surprisingly, an hour and half had gone by when they finally made it back to the car. Somehow, Carli had even persuaded him to pet the reindeer after all.

He studied her as they pulled back onto the expressway.

A little of the color had returned to her cheeks now that the car heater was fully on and blowing at them. Many of her wayward curls had escaped the tight band at the top of her head, and several dark tendrils framed her face. Why did she even bother putting her hair up? She'd been licking her lips and biting them after drinking the spiced cider. The abuse from her teeth turned them a pinkish red hue. He had an absurd urge to reach over and rub his fingers over her mouth to soothe them.

Damned if she hadn't been right. The little excursion had been a welcome respite from everything; he would even call it fun. That was the problem. It was way too easy to forget the world and just have fun with Carli Tynan.

He thought about what she'd said back there in the park. Her statement about starting new traditions. She was giving him way too much credit. He wouldn't even know where to start.

Her optimistic words just drove the truth home. They were too different. Trips to parks decorated with Christmas displays were all too common for someone like her. She had the kind of love and affection in her life that fully embodied everything that was good about Christmas. For him, Christmas was just another reminder of all he'd never had and never would.

CHAPTER SEVEN

"THIS IS IT," Carli said, and parked the car behind several others already in the driveway of a double structure colonial complete with a front porch and white picket fence. "Brace yourself," she warned. "Looks like everyone else is here too."

"Uh. Who would that be exactly?"

"Well, my two younger sisters live here. They're just teenagers. Marnie and Perri. Twins actually." She motioned with her chin to the white minivan. "Then there's my oldest sister, Tammy. That's her vehicle right there. Which means my nephew and brother-in-law must be here, as well. And that mini-coupe belongs to my other sister, Janie. She's about two years older than me. And I'm guessing her boyfriend came with her." The last statement held just a hint of tightness, lacking the soft quality he'd heard in her voice when referring to the other members of her family. He knew he hadn't imagined it. Something had happened between Carli and her next older sister.

Carli opened her door and stepped out of the vehicle. "And of course there's my mother and father."

He tried to count in his head all the names she'd just mentioned. How in the world was he going to keep track of all these people? Also, how did they all fit in that small structure?

"Come on. I'll make all the introductions inside," she told him, leaning back into the vehicle. "And you can get cleaned up. It's been a long ride, I know."

It had taken hours to get here. But Justin had to admit, it hadn't felt that way. In fact, he had to admit he was somewhat disappointed that his time alone with Carli in the car had come to an end. They'd decided to come straight to her home, as the delay of traffic made them even later. As much as he would have appreciated the time to stop by his room at the inn, he didn't want to risk being late and rude. Not an ideal first impression.

Though why he was so deeply concerned about Carli's family's perception of him was something of a mystery. He didn't plan on seeing any of these people again once this week was over.

Carli used her key and opened the front door. "Hello? We're here."

They stepped into a small but tidy living room. A large red sofa sat against the wall, covered with thick, plush cushions. A patterned throw rug sat atop the hardwood floor. Several toy trucks lay scattered throughout the area and down the hall. A Christmas tree without the lights turned on decorated the corner by the fireplace. It had to be the coziest looking room he'd ever stepped into.

"In the kitchen," someone called in response. Carli shook off her coat and indicated for him to do the same. She hung up both in a closet adjacent to the front door. He followed her farther inside. The aroma of rich seasonings and an appetizing mix of spices hung pleasantly in the air. He realized he was famished.

"Carli! You're here." A small woman with a broad smile approached them. Her apron had a cartoon picture of a large, red lobster wearing a Santa hat. It said Santa Claws in bold letters across the top.

Justin immediately saw the resemblance. Carli's mother had the same subtle features, the same deep brown colored eyes. She embraced her daughter in a tight hug.

"I'm so glad to have you home," the older woman said. Were those tears glistening in her eyes?

Carli cleared her throat and motion toward him. "Mom. This is Justin Hammond. He's uh…my boss."

Justin extended a hand. "Nice to meet you, Mrs. Tynan."

She ignored his outstretched hand and gave him a tight hug also. "Oh, you must call me Louise."

Justin awkwardly wrapped his arms around her shoulders. He tried to remember the last time he'd been bear-hugged by a middle-aged woman in a long apron, and couldn't recall a single time.

"Thank you for having me, Louise. Your home is lovely." In hindsight, he realized he should have brought some sort of house gift. How embarrassingly uncouth of him. He would have to pick something up in town. But visiting an employee's family in small-town Massachusetts was not his regular MO. He was a bit off his game here.

"Where are the others?" Carli asked, plucking a thick bread stick from a glass plate on the center of the table. She bit off the end and started chewing. Justin found himself momentarily distracted by the motion of her lips. He blinked and forced his attention back to her mother.

"Your father is out getting some groceries. Everyone else went for a quick walk," Louise answered. "Trying to wear out little Ray a bit. He wouldn't even take a nap this afternoon."

Carli smiled. "That sounds like our little Ray."

"He's very excited about his aunt Carli visiting. So it's partly your fault."

Carli laughed. "As if Ray needs an excuse to be overexcited."

"No, no, he doesn't." Louise turned to Justin. "Do you have any nieces or nephews?"

"No, ma'am. It's just me and my brother." Best to answer with a short and general response. No need to get into how Justin barely knew his own brother. Someone like Louise, with the family she had, would never understand the way he and James had grown up. On different sides of the coast. Hardly seeing each other, even on holidays or birthdays. It was the polar opposite of what Carli had grown up with.

"I've heard quite a bit from Carli about hers, though," he added, to turn the conversation spotlight elsewhere. "Can't wait to meet the little guy."

Though what he would say to a small child was beyond him.

Carli couldn't contain her laugh. As Justin's words left his mouth, a small blur in a puffy coat barreled through the kitchen and hurled itself into her.

"Aunt Carli! Aunt Carli! You're here. You're finally here!"

She kneeled down to Ray's height and wrapped her arms around her nephew. A swell of love and affection moved through her core. It never ceased to amaze her how much sheer emotion this child could invoke in her. Simply by the way he reacted whenever he saw her.

"Hey, little man." She tousled his hair. "I've missed you."

"I missed you too!" he said loudly.

Ray had no concept of an inside voice. Despite repeated attempts by all his elders to check him on it.

"You've grown," she observed and earned a huge smile.

"Momma says I'm a weed."

"You're growing like a weed. Let's see if I can even still pick you up." She gave an exaggerated show of false effort as she lifted him. "Oh, you're so heavy! This is probably the last time I'll be able to lift you."

"Prolly," her nephew agreed.

With Ray still in her arms, she turned to Justin. "I'd like you to meet a friend of mine."

Justin appeared confused. He lifted his hand before dropping it right back down to his side. Then he lifted his other hand and gave a small wave. He was trying to determine the right protocol when it came to meeting a kid. Carli had to hide her amusement at the thought. Why was he always so serious?

"Who is dis?" Ray asked, his dark eyebrows lifted in his small face.

"Don't be rude, Ray," Carli admonished. "This

is Justin Hammond. You should call him Mr. Hammond."

"Mr. Hammond," Ray repeated. Only his pronunciation and his missing teeth made it sound like ham bone. Carli couldn't decide whether to laugh or groan at that.

Justin stepped closer to the two of them. "Actually, I'd prefer it if you called me Justin. May I call you Ray?"

The child giggled. "Of course you can! It's my name!" he said with pride. Then to her horror, he added, "And your name is funny sounding."

"Ray..." Carli began but stopped when Justin laughed in response.

"My name is funny?"

Ray nodded. "Yup."

"What do you mean?" he asked with a curious smile.

Carli heard the other adults slowly make their way into the house as Ray wiggled in her arms.

"It's funny cause your last name has ham in it."

Justin lifted an eyebrow, seemingly deep in thought. "Hmm, that hadn't occurred to me. I suppose you're right."

Ray grinned. "Your first name is funny too."

Oh, sheesh. Now he was pushing it, Carli thought. Justin had zero experience with kids. He couldn't be expected to patiently listen to the silly ramblings of a four-year-old regarding the qualities of his name.

But he seemed to be playing along. "My first name too? How so?" he asked Ray.

"'Cause it sounds like something my mom says to me all the time."

"It does?"

"Yeah. Like she says 'Ray, it might be cold out. Put your coat on. Just in case.'"

Justin laughed out loud, and Carli couldn't help the humor that bubbled up from her throat either.

"Or she says 'There's your father. Just in time.'"

"Oh, Ray," Carli admonished, unable to keep the amusement out of her voice. "It isn't nice to make fun of people's names."

Ray turned to Justin. "I sowwy," he said, turning big chocolate-brown puppy dog eyes on him. Though he looked anything but. In fact, he looked plenty pleased with himself at the reaction he was getting.

To his credit, Justin turned serious in a very

fake way. "Well, you've certainly given me something to think about," he said.

The others strolled into the kitchen just then. Carli made the proper introductions after receiving a welcoming hug from her oldest sister, Tammy.

Janie, on the other hand, seemed hesitant to approach her. As was she hesitant to approach Janie. Carli hated this. She hated the distance that now seemed so insurmountable between them. Up until a year ago, they'd grown up as close as two peas in a pod. The expression on her mother's face said she was displeased too.

She dared a glance at Justin. He'd noticed the tension in the air between her and her older sister. That much was clear.

And then Warren entered. Carli's chest tightened, and her pulse pounded in her veins. She gave Janie's current boyfriend as polite a smile as she could muster.

"Carli, nice to see you again," Warren said, then went to stand next to Janie. Seeing the two of them so close together still didn't feel right, and she had to look away.

But she was over it all, Carli reminded herself. She had to be.

"Warren. Hello."

She motioned to Justin. "I'd like you to meet Justin."

The two men shook hands just as Ray shouted out, "I think that's Aunt Carli's boyfriend!"

Carli tried not to gasp in shock and horror as she set her nephew down. She didn't dare look in Justin's direction.

"Oh, my God!" Tammy exclaimed, then addressed Justin. "I apologize for my son's behavior. We are working on manners."

"No need for apologies," Justin assured her. Then surprised her by saying, "He's actually quite entertaining."

Carli took a deep breath. "No, that's not right." She corrected the boy. "I just work with Justin."

Ray simply shrugged. "Okay. Wanna see my new truck?"

The innocence of the question immediately ebbed Carli's annoyance. "Sure," she said, and tousled his hair once more.

Ray turned to Justin. "You come too," he ordered with a mischievous smile. Carli was just about to remind him to say please when he impishly added, "Just in case you like trucks too!"

Carli certainly wasn't kidding when she said dinner at her parents' place would be chaotic. Everyone talked over each other; multiple hands reached for various dishes. As the guest, he was offered each dish first. After that, it seemed to be a free-for-all.

Everyone participated in the rapidly changing conversation, even little Ray to the extent that he could. No one shushed the child, no one told him he was a messy nuisance when he dropped half his salad on the floor. In fact, they all actually laughed at the mess he'd created at the base of his chair. One of the twin sisters simply cleaned it up, gave him a peck on his chubby cheek, then sat back down to her dinner.

It was the loudest dinner Justin had ever sat through. It was also the most enjoyable. So different from the silent meals he'd had to endure as a child. If his mother even deigned to join him, that was. And this certainly beat the stuffy business dinners he regularly had to sit through.

Whereas this one had to be the loudest meal

he'd ever sat through, if anyone had asked him about that prospect a week ago, he would have said it sounded like a nightmare. So why in the world was he enjoying it so much?

"Justin, would you like another piece of lasagna?" Carli's mother asked.

He shook his head. "That would make it my third piece."

"So what's your point?" Carli's brother-in-law cracked from the other side of the table.

Her oldest sister poked the man in the ribs. "He's just saying that 'cause his average is about four servings each time Mom makes it."

Before Justin could answer, the twins started a mini tug-of-war in front of him with the last bread stick. It finally snapped in two, and for some reason they both thought that was the funniest thing and broke out in a peal of laughter.

Their little nephew joined in. Justin, in turn, couldn't help his own laughter. Apparently, a preschooler's giggles were highly contagious. Pretty soon, the whole table had broken out into laughter.

So this was what family meals normally looked like. A far cry from the silent dinners he and his brother shared around the television while their mom was up in her room wallowing in self-pity and their dad was still at the office. Back then, at least he hadn't been eating alone.

He hadn't even had that much after his mom had taken him away.

Carli watched as Justin laughed at something her brother-in-law told him by the hearth as they both sipped their after dinner coffee. Why was she not surprised that he had somehow fit so well in with her loud and boisterous family?

Sure, the Tynans had a way of making people feel welcome in their midst. But it was as if they'd all known him for years rather than having just met him. She'd daresay Justin seemed like he actually *belonged*.

She sighed. Probably just her imagination. Despite the circumstances, and despite the imminent danger he posed to the existence of her beloved store, Carli had to admit, deep down, he wasn't so bad. In fact, she might actually be growing quite fond of him.

Ray approached him right then and gave a tug on his pant leg. Justin immediately put down his cup and kneeled to hear what the boy had to say. The whole picture tugged at something within her chest, a longing she didn't want to examine in any way.

Carli made herself look away. What in the world was wrong with her? The man had simply had dinner with them. That's all that was happening here.

And a week from now, he'd be go back to being nothing more than a name on the company letterhead.

She turned to go back into the kitchen. As far as she could get from Justin and the picture he made in her family's living room.

Justin waited for Carli the next morning in the lobby of the Sailor's Inn Bed and Breakfast so that they could head over to the toy store. Overall the inn was a quaint, charming establishment unlike anything he would have encountered on the West Coast. The décor screamed New England, complete with a boat anchor hanging above a large hearth fireplace as well as the requisite ship in a glass bottle displayed in the center of the lobby.

Unbelievably, he was hungry. He didn't think he'd be able to eat for another week after the way Carli's parents had fed them last night. Louise had prepared enough food for an entire football team. Not that the numbers weren't damn near comparable. Carli had a large family.

As if reading his thoughts, or perhaps she'd heard his stomach grumbling, a matronly rotund woman appeared from the back holding a tray of steaming muffins.

"You weren't trying to sneak out without eating something first?" she asked.

She then smiled and set the tray next to a silver carafe on a side table against the wall. "I'm Betty Mills. My husband would have checked you in last night."

Justin shook her hand and introduced himself.

"Help yourself," she said, pointing to the tray from which drifted a delicious aroma of sweet sugary dough. "I've made vanilla almond and raspberry chocolate chip this morning. Plus, there's always the standard corn ones."

Justin's mouth actually watered. This certainly beat the dry granola bars he hastily grabbed on his way into work most mornings.

Betty laughed. "Or you can have one of each," she offered, clearly reading his mind once again.

The front door swung open behind them, and Carli walked through, bringing with her a gust of cold New England air.

Betty greeted her with a familiar smile. "Carli Tynan. So nice to see you back in town."

"Good morning, Betty. Justin." She glanced at the muffin tray. "I see you're taking good care of my friend here."

"I'd offer you some too, but I'm guessing Louise has handled that already?"

Carli patted her stomach and rolled her eyes. "She's been feeding me nonstop since I got here."

Justin couldn't take any more talk of food. He reached over and plucked one of the vanilla almond muffins, taking a big bite. A small burst of heaven exploded in his mouth.

He looked up to catch Carli watching him with a knowing smile.

"You're lucky to be here on vanilla almond day. Those are Betty's particular specialty. Though the cranberry comes in a close second."

"They go real well with a cup of coffee," Betty

said, pouring him some of the chicory-colored brew. "How do you take it?"

"Black, please," Justin answered and took the beverage from her. The heat from the ceramic mug warmed his hands. He liked his Seattle brew just fine, but the smell of this coffee sparked his senses.

"And what brings Mr. Hammond into town?" Betty asked.

Justin looked to Carli, unsure how to answer. How much was she willing to share with the town about the trouble that had brought the two of them here? He'd been in Westerson less than twenty-four hours and could already tell what a tight, close-knit community it was. Hearing about the potential closing of one of their businesses would probably not sit well.

And it certainly wasn't how he wanted to introduce himself.

To his relief, Carli answered for him. "Justin is here to visit his family's store." She offered no further details.

Luckily, Betty didn't push.

Moments later, they were out on the street

among scores of other pedestrians all bundled up against the harsh December air.

"Betty's quite the baker," Justin offered by way of conversation.

"Yes, quite." Carli seemed preoccupied. She had to be thinking about what he would say when after visiting the store. And how much credence his father would give it. He wished he could reassure her, he really did. But he'd been asked his professional opinion. He had an obligation to give it. Honestly and factually.

Even if it meant disappointing the woman next to him. Admittedly, that bothered him more than he cared for. Which made no sense. He had just met her a few days ago. This sense of familiarity and closeness that was developing within him had no basis in any kind of reality. Even so, he wanted badly to believe that it wasn't one-sided.

Several people waved and stopped them along the way to chat. Carli introduced him to everyone. At this rate, they would never get to Hammond's. She seemed to know every other person who walked by. Westerson wasn't the type of town where one could rush anywhere. Small talk and friendly conversation were a developed tal-

ent around here. A talent Carli had clearly perfected. She had kind words and a warm smile for
everyone who approached.

Until one man in particular turned the corner.
Carli's step actually faltered at the sight of him.
Justin immediately recognized who it was. He'd
met him last night at dinner. Warren, her sister
Janie's boyfriend.

All night, Justin had sensed a strange coldness
between the two of them. As if they were both
going out of their way to avoid each other. The
sister seemed just as uncomfortable when she
looked at them.

If he thought he was imagining it, the look
on Carli's face right now reaffirmed any suspi-
cion. Justin had no doubt that if it hadn't been so
blatantly obvious that they'd spotted him, Carli
would have ignored Warren and continued walking.

It was a strange dynamic for a family that otherwise seemed so devoted and close. Had Carli
expressed some sort of objection to her sister's
boyfriend?

Warren approached from the other direction.
He offered a small wave. Carli merely nodded in

his direction. To Justin's surprise they all kept right on walking. He'd been fully expecting to stop and say *something*, just as they had with so many others along the way so far. The whole thing made him wonder. Warren had seemed friendly enough last night. He was clearly good to the sister.

But there was no doubt. Whatever issues Carli had with the boyfriend, they seemed to run deep.

Carli had been enjoying the walk to the store. She really had. She'd missed this town. And strolling through the center of Westerson this time of year had always served to lift her spirits. It was doing so now.

Like every other year, the town council had spared no effort or expense with the decorations. Festive wreaths hung on each lamppost. The winterized bushes had been wrapped up like big presents or otherwise adorned with silvery tinsel and bright colorful ornaments. Her fellow townspeople knew how to do Christmas right, and she was glad to that was on display for Justin to see.

But her mood went south when Warren Mathews

turned the corner and made a beeline right to them. It had been uncomfortable enough to have him there at dinner last night. For a split second, Carli thought about pretending she hadn't seen him. But he was directly in their line of sight. She had to acknowledge him in some way. So she did, just barely.

"It's just a bit farther, past this corner," she told Justin, more so to break the awkward silence than to give him an ETA update.

Justin remained wisely silent about the non-exchange with Warren just now. She gave him a side-eye glance. His hair was dotted with a slight layer of snow, his strong neck wrapped in a different cashmere scarf. The coat he wore fit him perfectly. Every inch of him looked the competent, successful tycoon that he was.

It was impossible not to notice the double takes that every woman who walked by gave them.

He definitely stuck out in this small town.

At that thought, Carli gave herself a mental kick. This was so not where her focus needed to be right now. Not when they were on their way to the store so that Justin could make observations about the way it was run. About its very existence.

A nervous flutter spun in her gut about what his reaction might be. Last night he'd been warm and friendly, fitting in with her family easily. But his reputation as a no-nonsense, numbers-oriented businessman preceded him. She couldn't let herself forget why they were even here in the first place.

It would be a mistake to take anything for granted when it came to Justin Hammond.

He held the door open for her when they arrived at the store. The heat hadn't quite kicked in yet for the day; a slight chill still hung to the air. It was still early. Yet the shelves were neat, and the displays were cheery and festive.

A tooting whistle sounded overhead. Carli looked up just as a model toy train went past above her head on a hanging track. That was new. Justin looked up too, but he didn't seem impressed. Probably making a mental note of how much constructing it must have cost the company.

"So this is it, huh?" Justin asked.

"Yes. Everything's organized by age group." She explained the layout as they walked. "The toddler toys line the aisles up front. As you move back, you start to get into the board games and such for the older children. Followed by video games."

"Makes sense."

"There's a corner that houses all the reading materials, the Book Nook. And a café that serves coffee, juice and some basic pastries. Shall we start there?"

"Sure."

"Mr. Freider is probably setting up in the café," she informed Justin. "It's in the back." She motioned for him to follow.

The aroma of hot chocolate and freshly baked croissants greeted them as they approached the café counter. Several customers were already in line for a quick breakfast. A young lady she didn't recognize waited on them with a cheery smile. Carli breathed a sigh of relief that Justin was witnessing the early-morning traffic in the store.

She turned to him. "I'd just like to point out that despite the early hour, the store has drawn several customers already."

"You'd like to point that out, huh?"

"Yes."

"The problem is we don't know yet how many of them will actually purchase an item before they leave. Notice there's no one at the registers."

She waved her hand in dismissal at that suggestion. "It's still early. Besides, a lot of people come to look around and help make their child's wish list to Santa."

"Which they may very well go purchase elsewhere. Most notably, online."

She was about to object to that comment when Mr. Freider stepped out of the kitchen area carrying a pitcher of creamer.

"Carli! I've been expecting you." He brightened when he saw them.

He set his load down and offered a hand to Justin. "Mr. Hammond."

"Call me Justin, please."

Carli realized she was holding her breath. Goodness, she was so nervous on Mr. Freider's behalf. The poor man had no idea of the reason behind their impromptu visit into town.

He took Carli gently by the arm. "I'm so glad you've decided to visit again, dear. It's been way too long."

"You sound like my parents, Mr. Freider," she teased.

"I'm just glad you're here. I was worried that scoundrel was going to keep you away for good."

Carli could feel the blood drain out of her face. Justin gave her a curious look. The last thing she wanted to talk about right now was Warren Mathews.

She frantically scrambled around in her brain for a way to head off the topic immediately. But Mr. Freider wasn't having it. He was old school and had no qualms whatsoever about speaking his mind.

"I don't care what anyone says about how these things are meant to be." He shook his head with indignation and outrage on her behalf. "It's a disgrace the way Warren treated you."

Justin sat down next to Carli in the corner of the store she'd called the Book Nook. It was like being in a small book closet. The three surrounding walls were nothing but shelves of books. They were going through the several binders Mr. Freider had provided them about the store's numbers and operations. Dear heavens, the man hadn't even bothered to computerize any of the tracking data. How did he keep it all organized?

They'd started out in Freider's office, but there were just too many binders to go through and spread out. As a result, Justin felt ridiculous as all the chairs out here were clearly made for small children. Not to mention, customers were constantly stepping around them to peruse the books.

Still, Carli seemed to prefer being out here. And so far, they were both doing a remarkable job of conveniently ignoring Mr. Freider's cryptic comment earlier. It didn't mean Justin had stopped thinking about it, though.

A flash of anger surged through his chest. From what he knew of her so far, Carli was kind and soft hearted. Generous to boot. The thought of someone treating her badly or taking advantage of her made him want to crush something. Or to find the offender and personally make him answer for the transgression.

He gave his head a shake. How caveman of him. Again, none of this was really any of his business. His visit to Westerson would be a short one. He was only here to do a job.

To Carli's credit, she'd been right about the

flow of traffic into the store. And he had to concede that people were actually purchasing items at a fairly steady rate at the registers. Maybe there was hope for the location after all. Or maybe he was just trying to come up with ways not to disappoint the lady sitting next to him.

"Well, isn't this a déjà vu!" Mr. Freider approached them, carrying a tray of scones and hot coffee. "Carli Tynan, sitting at the Book Nook. It's like all these years haven't gone by at all."

He set the tray amid the pile of files and binders. "Thought you both might like some refreshments."

"Thanks," both she and Justin said in unison as they both reached for the same scone. He could have sworn an electric current shot through his arm clear to his chest at the contact. Carli looked up at him in surprise. Had she felt it too?

"Please, go ahead." Justin nodded toward the tray, but he continued to let his fingers linger on hers. Heaven help him, she made no attempt to remove her hand either.

Mr. Freider hadn't moved. He stood staring at the two of them, a curious look on his face. "There's plenty more where that came from."

He finally turned. "I'll let you two get back to work then."

Justin watched the older man walk away. "What did he mean exactly? About the whole déjà vu thing?"

Carli ducked her head slightly, didn't look up at him. "I spent a lot of time here as a kid. Guess I should admit that. Most of that time was spent right here in this very corner."

"I'm not surprised you were a big reader."

She turned to another page, her gaze still downward. "You have no idea. Sometimes it was the only escape."

He paused, wondering if he was being pushy. What exactly was the protocol under such circumstances? His curiosity won out. "How so?"

She gave a small shrug. "You've seen how loud and busy living in that house can be. It's always been that way. Sometimes I just needed to be away from it all."

Justin thought about that. He hadn't known anything but solitude. And here she was telling him she'd actually sought that out.

"It's not like it was really noticed when I was

gone," she added, shocking him. "As long as I returned home at a reasonable hour."

He waited in silence, giving her a chance to continue or stop. Though he was itching to know the truth behind that statement. He almost breathed a sigh of relief when she started speaking again.

"As you know, I was the middle child," she said, and highlighted an item on the page she was studying. "Sometimes, often, actually, that might be why I was easy to overlook."

"So you sought refuge here."

She nodded. "Books always gave me a whole other world to call my own. And even during the busy months, I always found it peaceful here." She finally looked up at him then. His breath caught at the depth of feeling shining in her eyes. "My sisters always had something that needed tending to. Tammy being the oldest was always on the brink of something new. The twins were so small, and they were double the work. And Janie...well, you've seen Janie." She blinked as if pushing away a thought. "My parents were always busy with one or all of them at once. I thought it best to just try to stay out of the way."

He didn't quite get her last point about her next older sister but didn't dare interrupt her.

"Me, I had my books at Hammond's Toys," she added.

Justin wanted to kick himself. He hadn't fully grasped her connection to this place. No wonder she was so invested in the success of the store. Still, he'd never, ever made a business decision based on anything but hard-core facts and data.

Logically, there was no reason to start doing anything differently now.

So why did he feel like such a lowly heel?

CHAPTER EIGHT

A CHILLY GUST of wind met Carli and Justin as they stepped outside later that afternoon. The light, barely noticeable flurries of earlier had turned into a steady snowfall.

Justin had tried really hard to focus on the plans for the store Mr. Freider had been discussing with them and on the figures he'd presented. But his usual sharp focus had failed him. He couldn't stop thinking about what the store manager had said to Carli. That Warren had somehow done Carli wrong. And then all the things Carli had revealed to him as they sat over the binders.

"Aunt Carli! Mr. Justin!" A child's voice rang out. Across the street, in what looked to be the town square, stood a short squat figure in a thick coat and a bright red hat. Ray. His mom sat reading on a bench a few feet away.

Justin felt an automatic and genuine smile.

Carli immediately started walking to them, and he followed.

"Hey, little man," she said when she reached her nephew. "What are you up to?"

His mother stood and gave them a warm greeting.

"We got some hot chocolate and a doughnut. And then I wanted to build a snowman. There it is." He pointed to a bowling-ball-size pile of snow in the center of the square. "I just started."

"He wanted to enter the snowman contest. But he was told he'd have to wait a few more years before being eligible," Tammy offered.

Ray's lip quivered. "It's not fair. Both Aunt Marnie and Aunt Perri are doin' it."

"They're quite a bit older than you." Carli looked up at her sister. "They've entered again, huh? Those two can't resist finding ways to compete with each other."

"Don't I know it."

Carli addressed Justin. "It never goes well. We'll just have to pray that neither one finals if the other doesn't."

Justin lifted an eyebrow in question. "Or?"

"Or you'll see fireworks in the middle of December."

Before he could comment, he felt a tug on his pant leg. "Wanna help me build a snowman, Mr. Justin?"

The question took Justin aback. He'd never actually built a snowman. Or a snow anything for that matter. Not even as a child. But how hard could it be? You just had to make three big balls of snow, then stack them.

He shrugged. "Sure, why not?"

Carli was staring at him with something akin to surprise on her face. "What?" he asked her. "Do you now doubt my snowman-making ability the same way you doubted my mechanical skills?" He wiggled his eyebrows at her in mock offense. That earned him a giggle from all three of his companions.

"Maybe we should hold our own little competition then?" he challenged.

"Yeah!" Ray chimed in, excitement ringing in his voice. "It'll be Aunt Carli and Mom against me and Mr. Justin. Boys against girls!"

"And who's going to judge?" Carli asked.

Ray looked over to the toy store. Mr. Freider

stood by the window working on a Yuletide display. He gave them a friendly wave. "Mr. Freider will!"

Justin held his hands up. "Wait a minute. We need some kind of wager, or it's hardly worth it."

"Losers have to shovel Mom's walkway after the nor'easter," Tammy offered.

"Agreed." Justin gave Ray a fist bump. "Let's get started."

About thirty minutes later, he was definitely regretting his decision. The women had a medium-height structure that they'd clothed with Carli's scarf and decorated with various items from Tammy's handbag. It sported a trendy pair of sunglasses and a bright hair bow.

He and Ray had barely managed to form two balls of snow, and the one they tried to put above the other kept rolling off. Ray looked to be on the verge of tears. But to his credit, he was trying to keep it together.

Justin knelt to his height. "Don't worry. I have an idea. Trust me, okay?"

Ray gave him a brave nod.

They called Mr. Freider out to commence with the judging. He took one look at the males' creation and crossed his arms in front of his chest. "Is your snowman laying down?"

"That's a snow turtle!" Ray informed him.

Mr. Freider bent closer to look at the two uneven balls of snow that Ray and Justin had pushed together. Two black pebbles sat atop the smaller one.

"Those are his eyes," Justin added, trying very hard to keep a straight face.

"I see." Mr. Freider rubbed his chin, deeply considering. He turned to the ladies' snowman, then back to their "turtle."

Ray actually looked nervous. The poor kid was probably holding his breath, Justin thought.

"I have a decision," Mr. Freider declared. "Anyone can make a snowman. But a Christmas turtle? Now that's something special. The boys win!" he said with a dramatic bow in their direction. Ray squealed in delight and ran over to give him a high five.

Tammy and Carli protested with outrage. But Mr. Freider stood firm. "I have made my decision." He shook Ray's hand and then Justin's to congratulate their victory.

It was right then that Justin felt something cold

and wet hit the back of his neck. Someone had just fired off a snowball! The culprit was no mystery. Carli had a distinctively smug look on her face. With no hint of guilt whatsoever.

Well, two could play at that game. He picked up a handful of snow and formed it into a tight ball, threw it right at her midsection. But she was too fast for him. She ducked to the side just in time. Then managed to pelt him with another snowball she'd prepared and had at the ready.

In moments, all five of them were ducking and launching snow at each other. Mr. Freider even joined in. Justin was marveling at the older man's accurate aim when Carli smacked him with yet another one. It landed on the side of his head that time. She clearly thought that was hilarious. Her laughter filled the air. Laughter at his expense!

That was it. Justin gave chase. He caught up to her by the side of the large gazebo that stood in the center of the square.

Grabbing her by the waist, he pulled her into his grasp from behind. She giggled and squirmed in his arms.

"You are not getting away. Sore loser."

"Let me go," she demanded, still laughing.

But then he turned her to face him. They stood nose to nose, his arms still wrapped around her middle. Her cheeks were rosy, eyes lit up with merriment. Her curly dark hair was in complete disarray, falling out of her wool knit cap.

She was the most stunning woman he'd ever laid eyes on.

He knew he should let her go. Knew they were in the middle of a very public square. But even under her thick coat, he could feel the warmth of her skin. The faint scent of her fruity shampoo tickled his nose.

He was too far gone; there was no way he would be able to stop himself from kissing her.

So he didn't even try to resist.

Carli's laughter died on her lips as Justin leaned in. Before she knew it, somehow his lips were on hers. Her breath caught in her throat at the contact. A heady shiver ran down her spine, clear to her toes. His lips were firm and warm against mouth. Just as she'd imagined. And she had imagined it.

And now here he was, holding her. Kissing her. This was insanity, complete foolishness. She was standing in the middle of Westerson town square in Justin Hammond's arms as they kissed. The taste of his mouth on hers felt like paradise. Every single cell along her skin tingled with desire. She'd been trying to fight it, but now there was no denying. She was attracted to him like she'd never been to any other man.

It scared her silly.

Justin was merely in New England for a business project. He had his own life, and his own business back on the West Coast. Oh, and there was also the small matter of him being heir to the company she worked for. She had to regain some sense.

With a sigh of regret, she made herself pull out of his grasp. Forcing herself to meet his eyes, she realized Justin looked just as shaken as she was.

A small hand tugged at the hem of her coat. "Hey. I thought you said he wasn't your boyfriend. Why you kissing him then?" Ray demanded.

Heavens, how in the world was she supposed to respond to the child? Not like she had any kind of real answer.

She looked away, desperate to come up with

something she could say. Only to find her sister staring at her, eyes wide with shock. Great, just great. There was no way this little event wouldn't be shared with every member of her family.

Mr. Freider muttered something about having to return to the store and walked away. She was certain she'd seen a hint of a smile on the his face.

Correction, Carli thought. The bit of news about Carli kissing her boss would be shared with every member of the town, not just her immediate family. How could she have been so reckless?

She took a deep breath, fighting to regain some composure.

Thankfully, her sister saved her from having to answer Ray when she walked up and lifted the boy into her arms. "Hey, you're looking pretty wet. Let's get you home and cleaned up."

Carli mouthed a silent *thank you*. The look her sister returned left no question that they would be discussing the matter in due time. Carli suppressed a groan at that prospect. Nevertheless, Tammy had just saved her from what would have no doubt been a cringe-inducing conversation with her nephew. Now, if only someone would save her from what was sure to follow with Justin.

Justin looked down out his window at Main Street Westerson. The late-afternoon sun shone glaringly on the thin blanket of snow that covered the town. And word was there was more snow expected. The forecast predicted a powerful nor'easter that really just sounded to him like an overblown snowstorm. If he'd experienced any during his childhood, he couldn't recall. Not that he would. He'd perfected the art of burying his childhood memories over the years.

He was way more focused on the storm that had been brewing inside him. He'd managed to get in a few hours of work, but it had been like swimming against the current. The events of the morning kept playing through his head.

The walk with Carli when she'd reacted so strangely to Warren as they'd encountered him. Mr. Freider's words about whatever had happened between the two of them.

The snowball fight. And what it had somehow inexplicably led to. The way Carli had responded when he'd kissed her.

Justin rammed a frustrated hand through his hair. This was useless. He wasn't going to get anything done when his mind was a jumble of thoughts about Carli.

The digital clock on his nightstand read close to five o'clock. A bit earlier than he normally liked to eat but getting dinner would at least give him something mundane to do. He'd noticed a charming mom-and-pop pizza joint this morning on the way to the store. And the walk would do him good. Grabbing his coat, he took the stairs to the first floor.

Almost everyone he ran into on his way either offered a friendly nod or a smile. Several said a simple hello. This was so not Seattle. Or any other city he'd visited over the years. The townspeople of Westerson were beyond friendly straight to outgoing. It explained Carli's personality somewhat. She was a product of this town.

Maybe it was just the approach of Christmas that had all of them behaving in such a manner. This atmosphere couldn't be a permanent characteristic, could it? He wasn't going to be here long enough to find out.

Either way, he was enjoying it now, but he

wasn't the type who could really fit into a town like this. Everyone knew each other. He preferred the anonymity of the big city.

He made it to the pizza parlor where an early crowd of hungry customers had already gathered. The rich aroma of tangy tomato sauce and yeasty dough made his stomach growl. He'd intended to get a slice or two but decided a whole pie might be in order.

Someone tapped him on the back as he stood in line.

One of Carli's younger twin sisters. "I thought that was you," Perri told him with a smile.

"Fancy meeting you here."

Her eyes narrowed on him with confusion. What a fuddy-duddy thing to say to a teenager. "It must be pizza Sunday in Westerson, huh?" he asked, motioning to the growing crowd.

"Nah, it's always this packed at Diammatta's. Plus there's a hockey game on tonight. Pizza and hockey go great together."

"I suppose they do."

"You don't watch hockey?"

"No, not really. I'm more of a baseball fan."

She shrugged. "Anyway, I hope this doesn't take too long."

"You have plans?" What was there for a teen to do in a town this small?

"I wanna go work on my snowman. For the competition over at the tree farm next week. They decide the winner on Wednesday."

"I heard about that. You and your sister both entered"

Perri rolled her eyes. "Don't know why she bothers. As if she could beat me." There was no animosity or spite in the way she said it. Just a healthy dose of youthful confidence.

"Pretty sure you'll win, huh?" he asked, then thought about his pathetic attempt earlier with Ray. That only had him remembering the kiss he'd shared with Carli.

Damn.

The pizza line was barely moving despite several people taking orders behind the counter. Not that he was in a rush; the only thing waiting for him was an empty hotel room and a bottle of beer from the mini fridge.

"Marnie doesn't stand a chance," Perri declared.

"She's been talking smack about it all week. I'll show her. Wait till you see my creation."

"I wasn't really planning on attending, actually."

She looked him up and down. "Well, why not?"

Justin shrugged. "I wasn't really invited."

"Well, consider yourself invited as of this very moment. By the likely contest winner, no less. Oh, and you should join us for dinner tonight too."

It struck Justin how poised this young lady was, how composed and confident. She'd met him two days ago. Yet she felt certain he would be accepted and welcome at her house for dinner, without having to run it by anyone else. Whatever Louise and her husband had done in raising their girls, they'd instilled in them a strong sense of self-worth. A rare thing these days.

The real question was, would Carli feel the same way about Perri's invitation? He had to admit, he really wanted to see her.

"Come on," Perri insisted. "Have pizza at our house."

He did owe the Tynan family a meal. They'd so graciously cooked for him his first night here.

The least he could do was reciprocate with pizza tonight.

"I'd love to. On one condition."

"What's that?"

"The pizza is my treat."

She grinned. "I can't think of a reason to turn that down."

Maybe not. But Carli probably might. Would she be angry that Justin had found a way to see her? It was a chance he was willing to take.

It took close to an hour, but they were finally out the door with several steaming boxes of thick crusty pizza with various toppings. Perri made them rush back to the Tynan house to keep them as hot as possible. Between the steam from the boxes and the near run, Justin was in a sweat by the time they reached the front porch.

Carli was the one who answered the door. The shock on her face at seeing him on the other side had him questioning the spontaneous decision to come.

"Look who I found at Diammatta's!" Perri exclaimed as they made their way in. "He's treating us."

Carli's mom and dad were already in the kitchen,

pulling out plates and cups. "How nice," both parents said in unison.

He noticed Carli didn't make eye contact as he moved past her to put down the pizzas. A whiff of her shampoo wafted to his nostrils, and his thoughts immediately went once again to the kiss they'd shared. It hadn't been his wisest move, but he'd hardly been thinking straight when he'd kissed her. Hell, he could barely think straight now with her just standing in the same room. He'd thought about that kiss all afternoon, had barely been able to focus on a conference call with his office assistant back home. The way she'd tasted, the way she'd felt in his arms. The way she'd responded.

He knew those things would haunt him for a good long while once he returned to Seattle. He was hardly likely to meet anyone else like Carli Tynan. That's why it made no sense that he was so damn attracted to her. Carli was nothing like the women he normally ran into. Most of the women he'd dated were practically carbon copies of each other. Wealthy, socialite types who could barely be bothered with much more than shopping for the next gala on their calendar.

He and Carli were from two different worlds. She had family, friends and a career she loved. Her Christmas party back in Boston showed she had the affection and respect of her colleagues.

Above all, she worked for his father, a man Justin wanted nothing to do with once this little project was over.

Yes, kissing her had been nothing less than foolish.

Finally, once slices were plated and drinks poured, Carli deigned to acknowledge him with a tight smile, albeit one that didn't quite reach her eyes. "You didn't have to spring for the pizza, Justin," she told him in a clipped voice.

"It was the least I could do after your family's been so gracious."

"It was really not necessary."

The exchange earned a shocked look from both her parents.

"That's just rude," Marnie admonished her, not holding back, like the younger sister that she was. "What she means to say is thank you."

Justin studied Carli's stern facial expression and the tight set of her jaw. Judging by her reaction since he'd first walked in, and the rigid set of her spine right now, she was far from thankful that he was here. In fact, she looked more than ready to toss him out on his behind.

Normally, Carli loved pizza from Diammatta's. Their pies were the best this side of the state. Tonight however, she could hardly taste any flavor. In fact, she may as well have been eating cardboard. No fault could be placed on the cook. It had nothing to do with the food but had everything to do with the man sitting across from her at her parent's kitchen table. She'd almost dropped in shock when she'd opened the door to find Perri standing there with him.

Her behavior bordered on being rude, she was well aware, barely having said more than a few words to him since he'd walked in. Luckily for her, both her younger sisters and parents were seasoned conversationalists.

But what was there for her to say? She could hardly make small talk, pretending that what had happened between them earlier today wasn't foremost in her mind. Justin was thinking about it too. She could tell by the way she caught him looking at her, how his gaze lingered on her lips whenever she took a bite. How in the world was she supposed to try to eat?

When all she could think about was if she would ever be kissed that way again.

Forget the fact that she worked for the company Justin was heir to. Men like him didn't fall for women like her. He was only in New England for a short-term project, one aspect of which she was desperately trying to get him to change his mind about. After that, he would be gone for good.

If she hadn't been able to maintain a relationship with someone she'd known for years and who had grown up in the same town, how could she dare hope to interest someone as worldly as Justin Hammond?

Blessedly, an hour later the dishes were finally cleared and the table wiped down. Carli was more than ready to show Justin the door. But then her father did the unthinkable. He invited Justin to stay to watch the hockey game.

Leaving her with no choice but to join them.

It would look suspicious to her parents to try to get out of it. She never missed watching a game with her father while in town. Her dad already had a roaring fire started in the fireplace when they all made it into sitting room. Normally, she would have grabbed one of the sofa cushions and plopped herself down in front of the flames as they cheered and shouted at the TV. But there was no way she was going to enjoy either the fire or any of the ice action tonight.

If any of her family members sensed her discomfort, they didn't show it.

At the end of the second period, she was more than ready to come up with an excuse and call it a night. But her father caught Justin staring at one of the framed sketches hanging on the wall.

Oh, no.

"Those make us proud of our girl's talent," her father boasted.

Justin raised an eyebrow in surprise. "One of your daughters drew that?"

Her father lifted his chin in a show of pride. "Sure did. That one sitting right there. The one who works for you."

Carli tried not to groan out loud. She did not want to talk about her portrait sketches with Justin Hammond. Especially not tonight. Then her father made it even worse when he added, "It's second-period intermission, Carli. Why don't you show him the others that are hanging around the house?"

Justin turned to her expectedly. She had no choice but to stand up. He followed her down the corridor.

"This one is of my two younger sisters," she said, pointing to a frame hanging near the kitchen hallway. It was a profile picture of Perri and Marnie about four years ago when they were thirteen or so.

She tried to move on, farther down the hallway where a portrait she'd drawn of her mother hung. But Justin stopped her with a hand on her arm.

"Carli, wait."

She stopped in her tracks, but couldn't look him in the eye.

"First of all, these are amazing," he stated, motioning to the sketch on the wall. "I'm no expert but even to a novice it's clear you have a real talent."

She inhaled a deep breath, oddly touched by the compliment. It wasn't anything she hadn't heard before, but somehow coming from him... It just felt *more*.

"Thank you. It was just a hobby I had a while back."

"You had?"

She shrugged. "I haven't drawn in a while. I have my reasons." Reasons she had no intention of getting into with him of all people.

As far as she was concerned, the last sketch she'd started would be her last one. The only one she'd ever torn to shreds.

Justin looked as if he was ready to question her further but apparently changed his mind. Must have been her closed expression.

"Second," he began, "I know I should I apologize for what happened this morning. In the town square." He took a deep breath before continuing. "But I'd be lying if I said I was sorry."

Well, that was certainly a straightforward and honest statement. She had no idea what to make of it, however. What exactly did he mean? That mistakes happened? Did he even consider it a mistake?

"I think we should just move past it," she blurted out, too tired and too frazzled to analyze any of it further. The truth was, she would welcome his kiss even now. As ridiculous as it was, part of her wished he would take her in his arms right here in the hallway.

"Move past it?"

She nodded with emphasis, though not entirely certain exactly what she was arguing for. "It was a fluke, right? We were both having fun and then things just took an unexpected turn. Nothing more."

Justin stepped closer, so close she could see the hint of shadow that had appeared on his chin since this morning. The scent of his aftershave wafted to her nose, and she had to resist the urge to lean into him and take a deeper sniff.

"So you'd like to just forget it happened."

Carli's answer was interrupted when the front door swung open and Tammy walked in with Ray in tow.

"Aunt Carli. Mr. Justin," Ray squealed when he saw them and made a beeline to where they both stood.

"Aunt Marnie texted that there was pizza. I love pizza!"

Carli took the interruption as a chance to catch her breath, thankful for her clueless nephew's disruption. Things with Justin were getting just a tad too intense. She didn't think she'd be able to give him the same nonchalant response if he asked her about the kiss again.

"Did you guys save me any?" Ray asked with a hint of panic in his voice, as if it just occurred to him that there might not be any pizza left.

"Of course we did," Carli reassured him. "Your favorite, extra cheese. Let's go get you some."

She reached for her nephew's hand and started to lead him to the kitchen.

Justin cleared his throat. "I guess I should get going. I haven't answered any emails all day, and it's already eight o'clock."

Ray stopped in his tracks and turned to him, clear disappointment etched in his small face. "Do you really have to go, Mr. Justin?"

Carli felt a little taken aback. Ray was clearly developing a fondness for him. In the span of two short days, Justin had already made an impression on the little boy. Her heart sank. It was no wonder. Besides Carli's father and his own dad, Ray was surrounded mostly by women. Another man around was probably a real novelty for him. He was going to be heartbroken when Justin left. Add that to the list of casualties when

Justin walked out of their lives for good in less than a week.

Justin leaned over to Ray's height. "I'm afraid so."

"Can you come over tomorrow? Aunt Carli and I are baking cookies."

Carli groaned inwardly. She'd promised Ray on the phone they would make a batch of Christmas cookies, then spend part of the day decorating them.

Why did her family keep inviting Justin to events? First Perri, now Ray.

She couldn't exactly rescind the invitation. Even if had just come from a four-year-old.

"I would," Justin answered, "but I'm not much of a cook."

"That's okay. I can show you what to do. Please?" He gave Justin a big, toothless grin. "Me and Aunt Carli could teach you how."

Justin looked up and met her eyes above her nephew's head. "I'd like that," he said. "I'd like that a lot."

CHAPTER NINE

CARLI TOSSED AND TURNED. Her bedside clock said it was 12:30 a.m. This was the same bed she'd slept in as a teenager. Right in this very room. She was never uncomfortable here. Not even during all those years of dramatic teenage anguish. But tonight was a different story. She couldn't find a comfortable position. And she couldn't seem to fall asleep.

Her thoughts kept returning to the man about three blocks away at the Sailor's Inn Bed and Breakfast. Was he fast asleep as was likely at this hour? Or was there a chance he was thinking about her?

He'd seemed genuinely interested in her artwork. But she wasn't quite ready to talk about that yet.

She needed sleep. But it was no use. Huffing out a breath, Carli got out of bed and put on her slippers. She walked over to the window and lifted the blind. She could see the rooftop of the B and B from where she stood. From there, her imagination took over. She thought of Justin in his bed, under the covers. A man like him probably slept with only pajama bottoms. Or nothing at all.

She sucked in a breath at that thought and tried to force the image out of her head.

This was the closest she'd ever come to fantasizing about a real actual man in her life. Not even with ex-boyfriends had she done such a thing. But here she was, in the dead of night, unable to get Justin Hammond out of her mind. A curse escaped her lips on a whisper. Damn him for kissing her the way he did. And damn her for responding. What a mistake. She should have never gotten playful with him in the first place. Why, oh, why hadn't she just said hello to her nephew and then walked away when she'd seen him in the town square? If only she could go back in time and stop herself from throwing that snowball.

It was such a ridiculous thing to wish for that she couldn't help but laugh. To think, an ill-timed snowball fight had led to such turmoil within her.

She would have happily gone on with her life, admiring Justin from afar. But now there was no turning back from the line she had crossed. And that's exactly what she'd done—crossed a line.

Well, maybe there was no turning back time or rectifying the mistake she had made. But she could certainly vow to be more cautious in the future. From now on, for the week or so that she and Justin were in Westerson, she would be the utmost professional. She wasn't one of those women to wallow in her mistakes, but she certainly made sure to learn from them.

Starting tomorrow morning, Justin would see nothing but the serious and accomplished career woman that she was. She'd make sure to steer the conversation toward business matters and details surrounding the store and its operations.

She just had to figure out how to do that exactly, while baking Christmas cookies with the man all day. Right. Easy-peasy. Carli sighed and walked over to the bookcase in the corner of her room. Plucking out one of her childhood favorites, she settled back onto the bed and opened the well-worn pages to one of her preferred chapters.

May as well read, she thought. There was no way she was going to fall asleep anytime soon.

The smell of newly baked muffins and freshly brewed coffee hit Justin as soon as he left his room. Betty was already pouring a cup when he reached the small dining room.

She handed it to him. "I heard you coming down the stairs," she told him with a bright warm smile.

Justin blinked as he took the cup and uttered a heartfelt thanks. He couldn't remember a time someone had listened for him in the morning just to have a cup of coffee ready. No doubt Betty was simply being an attentive innkeeper. Still, he felt oddly touched by the gesture.

She handed him a napkin as he sat down at one of the small linen-covered tables.

"I also baked more of those vanilla almond muffins that you liked so much," she told him offhandedly.

Justin felt his mouth water at that bit of news. He was going to gain so much weight this week. "But I thought those were only made on Saturdays?"

"Normally. But you seemed to enjoy them so much. I wanted to make them for you again."

Justin felt an odd sensation at the base of his throat. Perhaps Betty really was simply responding to the tastes of a paying customer. But this was a novel experience for him. The large chains and glamorous hotels he usually stayed in offered the utmost in glitz and luxury. But no one had ever gone out of their way to specifically make something just because he'd liked it.

Hell, no one would have even noted such a thing, even in one of the establishments where he was a regular, highly regarded guest. The notion left him with an unexpected sense of familiarity. "I know you must be busy, Betty, but do you have a minute or two to join me?"

She didn't hesitate and pulled out a chair. "That would be lovely, thank you. It will give me an excuse to put off the myriad of items on my to-do list this morning."

"Glad to oblige," he said, and gave her a conspiratorial wink.

"And what are your plans for the day?" she asked him.

Justin grabbed one of the muffins and split

it open. Aromatic steam arose from the center. "Unbelievably, I'll be baking Christmas cookies."

Her smile grew. "Why is that so unbelievable?"

He swallowed. "It's nothing I've ever done before. Nor ever expected to do."

Betty's eyebrows drew together. "You've never baked Christmas cookies? Not even as a child?"

He wasn't aware it was so unheard-of. The truth was, his mother hadn't been the baking type. Heck, she hadn't really been the *mother* type in any way. There were always baked goods and pastries laying around in the various kitchens he'd been in over the years, but he'd be hard-pressed to say where they'd come from.

"Well, I imagine the Hammonds had plenty of people on staff to bake for them. I guess it makes sense that you never did so yourself."

Justin wasn't going to get into the whole Christmas conversation and tell this kindly woman that cookies were the last thing on his mind whenever the holidays came around. And then when he and his mother had left New England, it had just become another day.

Christmas celebrations were a family affair for most of the world. He had a brother, but he may as well have been an only child. And even the parent he'd grown up with had barely been around. Very different than the way Carli had grown up, for instance.

"So how'd you get corralled into it then?" Betty asked.

"A very persuasive four-year-old," Justin answered, hardly believing it himself. It was difficult to say no to that little nephew of Carli's.

She laughed at his answer. "I should have known. Ray can be quite persuasive when he wants something," she said, echoing his thoughts.

"He certainly had my number."

He didn't tell her that there was more to it. Or about how he knew he'd be spending this Sunday alone otherwise. How he'd jumped at the chance to be able to spend it with Carli. Even doing something as mundane as baking cookies.

Betty somehow seemed to read his thoughts yet again. "Mmm-hmm. And tell me, was Ray the only reason you agreed to do this?"

He lifted an eyebrow in question, though he obviously knew what she was getting at. The woman was very perceptive, it appeared.

"I just thought I'd give it a try."

She wasn't falling for it. "I see. And it had nothing to do with the way you were looking at Carli Tynan yesterday morning, I suppose."

Wow. Was everybody in this town so direct? He bit down on another piece of muffin as he tried to scramble for a way to respond.

"I'm sorry," Betty began, sparing him. "It's just that I've known that girl since she was knee-high. One of the sweetest, purest souls you'll ever meet. She doesn't deserve to have her heart broken."

Again. Though unspoken, the word hung in the air as clear as day between them. Then the older woman suddenly stood up with a soft clap of her hands. "Oh, dear. I hadn't realized how late it was getting. I really should get to those chores. Please excuse me."

"Of course." Justin stood, but she'd already turned away and was walking to the front desk.

Leaving Justin with the succinct feeling that, sweet old lady or not, he'd just been issued a gentle yet clear warning.

Carli opened the door to him with a yawn, then stepped aside to let him in. She was dressed in baggy gray sweatpants, an oversize flannel shirt and thick fuzzy socks. Her hair was pulled back in a loose ponytail at the base of her neck but several tendrils had made a blatant escape and framed her face haphazardly.

She looked downright adorable.

What was wrong with him? Justin thought as she took his coat and hung it. He'd been less attracted to women wearing scanty lace panties than he was to her right now. None of it made any sense.

He glanced around the empty house. "Where is everyone?"

She stifled another yawn and shook her head. "Sundays are pretty busy around here."

"I see."

"My parents are out running errands after services, the twins had breakfast plans with friends. And Tammy's due to drop Ray off. But she's always late, usually because it can be a military level challenge getting a four-year-old out the door. Particularly on a Sunday when *The Squigglies* are on."

"*The Squigglies*?"

"Ray's favorite TV show."

He followed her to the kitchen. "Can I get you some more coffee? Though I'm guessing Betty has already filled you up to the brim."

People in this town really seemed to know each other well. "Correct call."

"Just as well. I might actually need the full pot for myself," she said through yet another yawn.

"Long night?"

She didn't look at him as she poured her coffee. "I didn't get much sleep. Sometimes I have trouble sleeping right before a big storm hits."

For some reason, her statement didn't quite ring true. "I've never heard of that. Weather-induced insomnia."

She glared at him over the rim of her coffee cup, so intensely that he had to stifle a laugh. So what was the real reason for her insomnia? What were the chances it had anything to do with him? He was most likely just flattering himself. But it was an intriguing notion. Lord knew he'd spent more than a few waking moments overnight remembering that kiss. The way she had felt in his arms, the warmth of her body up against his. The way she'd tasted.

He cleared his throat. "So tell me, just how

bad is this storm supposed to be? When is it due even?"

She swallowed the gulp of coffee and sighed with pleasure as it went down. The whole image sent a surge of longing through his chest. He gripped the granite counter in front of him just to give his hands something to do.

"Well, it's a nor'easter. Set to bring several inches of snow with high, gusting winds. And of course, out here on the Cape there's always the real risk of flooding."

Justin recalled nasty storms from his childhood in Metro Boston. The way he'd hide under thick blankets as the wind rattled the windows. But not much else. He must have blocked it out. Too bad there was no real way to block out everything.

"And it's due to hit sometime tomorrow night." Carli answered the second part of his question.

"No one seems terribly nervous."

She shrugged. "Winter storms are a way of life around here. Some things you just can't change." She gave him a pointed look.

Wasn't that the truth? If he could, he would change the way he was starting to feel. Carli had awakened a longing within him that he hadn't known existed. More than his attraction to her physically, it was her warmth, her humor, the way she interacted with her family and friends. The combination was like a gravitational pull that seemed to suck him into her orbit. It made no sense; he would have to get over it. Carli deserved someone with the same sense of belonging and roots that she'd known all her life. He was too far removed from being such a person.

He'd remember kissing her for the rest of his life; that tender, sweet moment would live with him from now on. A cherished memory of a woman who could never be his.

"I guess not," he answered. Such a simple response. It warranted no further conversation. Nothing more needed to be said. On the surface anyway.

If he could tell her everything, if he could bare his soul, he'd admit that right now he wanted nothing more than to repeat the mistake he had apologized for. He wanted to pull her up against him, right here in her parents' kitchen and taste her plump soft lips. He wanted to run his fingers through her hair and feel her warmth.

No, he couldn't come out and say all that. But

there had to be a way to somehow convey how impressed he was of the woman Carli Tynan was. Or how fond he'd grown of her in such a short time, even though it couldn't lead to anything more.

He was trying to come up with the words when they were interrupted by the shuffle of small feet running through the house toward the kitchen.

Any further revelations would have to wait.

Justin Hammond had no idea how to separate an egg. Carli had to hold in her laughter as she watched him crack it open then stare blankly at it in his hands, clearly trying to figure out how to get the yoke apart from the rest.

When he reached for a spoon to do heaven knew what, she figured she'd better intervene in the interest of avoiding a food-borne illness.

"Here, let me help."

He looked so grateful that she had to suppress another laugh. Between Ray and Justin, she'd be hard-pressed to decide which one of them was less useful in the kitchen. So far, she might have to say it was Justin. As if to challenge that conclusion, her nephew chose that moment to knock over a bowl of sifted flour, making a colossal mess on the floor.

"Oops."

Carli sighed. Something told her they'd be heading to the bakery or they'd have to do without Christmas cookies this year. Her parents were both still out on their errands. Tammy had begged to run to the nail salon while they watched Ray. Maybe she should just call one of them now and have them pick up a box from Patty's Pastries on their way home.

She was debating whether to pull out a broom and dust pan or a vacuum when Justin somehow managed to drop both parts of the egg right into the pile of flour Ray had just spilled.

"Oops." This time, both males said it unison.

Carli didn't know whether to cry or just run out of the room screaming. Let someone else deal with all this.

Of course, that wasn't an option. She grabbed a large kitchen towel and threw it at Justin. "You work on the egg that got on the counter. While I try tackle the mountain of flour on the floor."

An hour later, they hadn't even managed to put anything into the oven. Yep, no doubt about it. Someone was going to have to make a bakery run.

The entire kitchen was a disaster area. She'd seen neater construction sites in Metro Boston. But just to go through the motions, for Ray's sake, she walked into the pantry where her mother kept the holiday themed cookie cutters. As if any of their creations would actually be viable enough to hold any kind of shape. Except for perhaps one mound of sugar cookie dough, they were batting zero.

A loud clanging sound followed by Ray's horrified scream had her dropping the cutters and running back out into the main area.

"What happened?"

Ray's lip quivered as he looked up at her. Justin seemed at a complete loss. Half the counter and part of the floor were covered in a shiny puddle of green.

"I don't really know," Justin began. "We were trying out the food coloring, trying to decide which color to use."

"I dropped the whole bottle," Ray wailed. Large fat tears began to roll down his cheeks.

Carli immediately ran to him.

"It was my fault," Justin said, ramming his hand into his hair. "I shouldn't have let him play with it."

Ray climbed off the counter stool he'd been standing on and ran straight into her arms. "I made a mess, Aunt Carli. And now we have no cookies."

Carli didn't doubt that the latter statement was the real cause of all the tears. She brushed them off his wet, ruddy cheeks.

"Oh, buddy. It's okay. It was just an accident."

Justin swiftly crouched next to them both. "Ray, it was my fault. I should have known better. Please don't cry."

For an insane moment, Carli had the thought that Justin might need comforting even more than the child. He seemed really shaken. He'd clearly never been around a crying child before. Heaven help them, he didn't realize they did it all the time.

Or was there something else behind his inflated response to the minor disaster?

Ray hiccupped on another sob.

"Hey, we'll still have some cookies," she reassured him. "This is no big deal." She spoke over his head, looking straight into Justin's eyes.

Her mother chose that moment to walk in. Taking in the scene, she blew out a deep breath. Then she went over to her grandson. Ray pulled away and ran to his grandmother as soon as he saw her.

"I ruined the cookies, Nana."

"Mmm-hmm. And the kitchen is a mess," she said in an even, soothing tone. "But it's nothing that can't be fixed. Okay?"

Ray sniffed and nodded.

"Let's go get you cleaned up," she said, and picked him up.

"Thanks, Mom!" Her mother could comfort Ray like no one else could.

"Don't thank me," Louise threw over her shoulder as she walked out with her grandson. "Just get that mess cleaned up. Both of you."

"Yes, ma'am."

Poor Justin looked like he'd just run through a minefield. "So that went well."

He blinked at her. "Where do we start?"

She pointed to the one ball of dough on the counter that had somehow survived, albeit it was the color of a mossy lake. "I say we try to salvage that dough so that we can throw at least one batch in the oven. Then we start scrubbing."

"You still want to bake? Using that dough?"

"Sure. Why not?"

"For one thing, it's green. Very green."

She shrugged. "So, we'll have green cookies."

"Uh-huh."

"Are you okay?"

He ran a hand through his hair. "I'm not sure. The little guy was pretty upset."

"He's four. It doesn't take much. He'll forget about the whole fiasco by bedtime."

"He will?"

"Of course."

"If that's true, it will be thanks to you. And the way you handled it. Your mom too."

"How else would I have handled it?"

He gave her a blank, confused stare. "You were just so... I don't know...gentle. And understanding." He took a deep breath. "And your mother was the same. Even as she agreed that the cookies were ruined, she calmed and reassured him."

"That's what one does when it comes to children. They're just learning their way."

"I guess I wouldn't know."

Carli grabbed a roll of paper towels and tore off a good amount. The green was starting to settle into her mom's granite counters. She handed a few to Justin, who followed her lead and began wiping furiously. "Maybe not. But you were a child once."

He snorted. "Trust me when I tell you, I don't ever recall any adult behaving quite so evenly after a major mishap. Or even in general."

Carli's heart nearly burst in her chest. How could that be? "You don't?"

Justin shook his head. "No. When I did something wrong, which was often, I got a thorough lashing of the tongue. Followed by some form of punishment. Then my mother would make sure my dad heard about what I did and what an awful handful I was, usually the moment he got home. That always led to loud, long arguments with plenty of door slamming."

"Oh, my God." She stilled. "Justin, that sounds terribly unfair."

"It's how I remember. I suppose a lot of it was my fault. I should have tried harder."

"You can't be serious. You were a child."

"Still, I was aware enough to realize my behavior was causing strife."

"Like every other child."

He shook his head. "Not really. Not James. I can't ever recall him acting out. It was always me."

"I'm sure James had his moments. It's just that some children are more active than others."

"Maybe. My behavior had ramifications for him too. He'd always turn tail and hide in his room whenever it started. I knew he was angry with me for causing so much trouble."

Carli's heart sank. She wanted to cry for the little boy Justin must have been. She doubted he was anything more than an energetic and curious child like so many others. Apparently, his parents used that as an excuse to vent their own issues and anger. To make it all worse, the two brothers had apparently turned on each other as a result.

He took another deep breath before adding, "So I know he must have blamed me for the destruction of our parents' marriage."

"How can that be?"

"On some level, he's right."

"Don't say that. A mere child can't cause the breakup of a marriage. There has to be underlying issues at play."

"You're right. But I caused the final fight that led to my mother reaching her last nerve, so to speak."

"What happened?"

Justin was wiping the counter, not looking at her as he spoke. The events he was recalling happened years ago, but they seemed to have left considerable if invisible scars.

"It was Christmas Eve. The big tree had been set up in the main foyer. I couldn't stop admiring it. It was so majestic. Bright lights and shiny ornaments. And it was so tall, I could barely see the top."

Oh, no. Carli could guess where this was going.

"I remember one particular ornament. Just out of my reach. A Red Sox catcher's mitt. It looked more like a toy. I just wanted to play with it for a bit. I was going to put it right back. But when I jumped up to grab it, the whole tree fell over. Almost all the ornaments broke."

"Oh, Justin. You must have been so scared."

"You have no idea. I came so close to running out the door in that moment. Thought maybe I could just keep running and never go back."

Carli noticed he'd bunched up the paper towels into a tight ball, gripping it in his fist.

"But my mother came rushing down the stairs. She kept yelling over and over how I'd been told so often to leave it alone. And why couldn't I just listen. She called my father and demanded he come home right then."

Carli's gasped in horror at the woman's reaction. To a simple accident that could have very well severely injured her son. She'd never wanted so badly to give another adult a reassuring hug. To hold him and tell him he'd done nothing wrong all those years ago. If anything, he'd been the one who'd been betrayed and disappointed. But though her arms itched to hold him, she clenched her muscles instead. It was doubtful Justin would want her sympathy. He seemed way too proud for that.

"What ensued when he arrived is not a pleasant memory," Justin continued.

"I'm sure it wasn't." She figured he didn't have

too many pleasant memories based on what he was revealing to her right now.

"I was young, but I remember the expression on James's face. He'd turned white as a ghost. I'll never forget what he said later that night. We could hear our parents having it out upstairs. He just walked over to me and gave me a hard shove. I couldn't blame him. He was so angry."

Carli was afraid to guess and almost didn't want to ask. But she had to. "What did he say?"

"He said he hated me."

She couldn't help it. Walking over to where he stood, Carli rubbed a soothing hand along his arm. He'd gone tight and rigid.

"That was the last time I saw him until we were well into our teens. Simply coincidentally at some boating event on the Charles. And didn't see him again after that for years."

What a burden to bear as a child, Carli thought. Justin had been too young to understand that his parents' tumultuous relationship hadn't been his fault.

"You can't believe you were the real cause of their divorce."

"I know that now. But for years I kept replaying that day in my mind. If only I had just left the tree alone."

"You were a child." She wanted to just say it over and over again until it somehow sunk into his psyche.

"Maybe. But I was old enough to know better."

"You can't honestly believe that. Sooner or later something was going to happen that triggered the same result—your parents didn't want to be together."

He gave her an indulgent smile. "Interesting theory. I always wonder though."

"Wonder about what?"

"What would have happened if I hadn't been their son. After all, I seemed to be the cause of all the animosity. If it wasn't for me, they probably would have been the perfect family who had everything. But then I came along."

Carli could no longer stop herself. Her arms automatically went up and went around Justin's wide shoulders in a tight embrace. They stood that way silently for several lengthy moments. There didn't need to be any words between them. Right now she just wanted him to feel her understanding and her support, wishing with all her heart that someone had done the same years ago when he'd been a small boy.

A boy who thought his family hated him.

CHAPTER TEN

JUSTIN WANTED TO kick himself. He hadn't meant to get into the whole sordid story of his childhood and what had led to him and James growing up on opposite coasts. But he'd just been so struck and so touched at how she'd gently dealt with Ray just now. Plus, it was so easy to talk to her. He'd be hard-pressed to say why that was. Never before had he divulged so much of his past to anyone, let alone a woman who he'd essentially just met.

He was usually much more restrained, more in control. But what little of it he had snapped like a stretched rubber band when she wrapped her arms around him and held him against her. This felt right; *she* felt right. He could smell the perfumed scent of her soft, delicate skin. Mixed with the hint of sweetness in the air, it shook his senses.

He had to taste her again.

Lifting her chin, he watched as desire shaded her eyes. She had the longest lashes. Her lips were lush and beckoning. He knew what he was about to do wasn't wise. He was technically in this town as her boss on a project. He had no business kissing her. Even as that thought ran through his head, he reached down and took her lips with his own.

She tasted as good as he remembered. No, even better. Like honey and forbidden fruit. He thought he might lose his mind when she responded. With a soft sigh against his mouth, she molded herself tighter against the length of him.

Unlike in the square, this time they were alone. The knowledge brought a heady sense of excitement that he found difficult to clamp down on.

Placing his hands against the small of her back, he pulled her even closer. He wanted her to feel his full reaction. She had to know how attracted he was to her. More than he'd felt for any other woman. Inexplicable on every logical level, but there it was.

But it was more than a physical attraction. He'd just opened up to Carli Tynan like no one else before. Her response had been to try to comfort him, to reassure him with both her words and her touch.

Her hands went up to his shoulders and she gave him a small nudge back, and he pulled away from the kiss.

"We really shouldn't be..." she whispered against his mouth.

"I know." But he guided her with his body up against the counter and kissed her again, deeper. She gasped in shock but didn't try to stop him.

If anyone had told him last week he'd be standing in a rustic New England kitchen kissing a Hammond employee, he would have laughed in their face.

The wisest thing to do would be to pull away. On top of everything else, they were in her parents' kitchen for heaven's sake. That reality was driven home when they heard the water turn off upstairs just as someone walked in through the front door of the house.

Carli jumped back and jerked out of his arms. She ran around to the other side of the kitchen island, clearly putting distance between them. Rubbing her lips, she averted her eyes.

Justin ran a hand down his face. How had

things between them gotten so heated, so out of control? He'd just barely delivered an apology for the first time he'd kissed her.

"I don't know how that happened," he began before Carli held up a hand to stop him.

Her sister Tammy entered the kitchen at that very moment. She stopped in her tracks as soon as she took in the scene. Justin tried not to groan out loud as Tammy's gaze traveled from her sister to him, then to the mess in the kitchen before landing back on Carli's bewildered face.

"You have some 'splainin' to do," she addressed her sister.

"Yes, she does," another voice chimed in as Carli's mother walked in. "Carli Tynan. That food coloring is going to leave permanent green stains on my counter. Why in the world have you two not cleaned it all up yet?" she demanded to know and then gave Justin a scolding glare for good measure. He squelched an urge to actually step back.

And now he was standing in that same style kitchen being reprimanded by the Hammond employee's mother. The whole scenario could be straight out of a sitcom.

Carli looked like she didn't know whether to laugh or cry. He felt pretty torn himself.

"This is all my fault."

Carli actually stomped her foot. "No, it's not. It just happened. Ray spilled the food coloring by accident. No one is at fault." She emphasized the last word.

Tammy gasped while Carli's mother tilted her head. "I must not have made myself clear," Louise said. "All I care about is that it gets cleaned up. Now."

"Yes, ma'am," they both said in unison. Tammy's sisterly smirk was undeniable as she followed her mother out of the room.

Carli let out a deep sigh as she watched the other two women leave. Grabbing the paper towels off the counter, she tore off a bunch before throwing the roll to him without warning. He caught it as it landed on his chest.

"Justin?"

"Yes?"

"You are really bad at making cookies."

Forty-five minutes later, Carli pulled the final tray of cookies out of the oven and set them on a rack to cool. They were definitely the greenest sugar cookies she'd ever seen.

Justin leaned over and gave them a long look. "They don't look like sugar cookies."

She didn't care. She just wanted this whole afternoon to be over. Also, she wanted to stop dwelling on the way Justin kissed.

"They look more like mint cookies," Justin added. He was right.

"Or perhaps spinach," she said, and earned a snicker.

They'd worked mostly in silence as they'd baked and cleaned. Everyone else seemed to have left. Traitors. No one had wanted to stay and help clean the mess. Not that she could blame them. Her mother's counter and a good portion of her floor tiles still held a greenish hue.

"All that matters is how they taste," she told Justin, poking one of the star-shaped cookies. Though it was still hot, she gingerly picked it up and tasted a small piece. "See, they taste great." She held it up to him. "Try it."

Justin's reached to take it from her. The touch of his hand on hers triggered another fiery tingle along the edge of her skin. Dear heavens, she was a fool. She had to fight this crazy attraction. He would be gone from New England and out of her life within a week. She worked for his family business. What was she doing kissing the man and then fantasizing about it afterward?

She had to get out of here.

"We should head to the store," she blurted out.

"The store?"

"Yeah, Hammond's Cape store. The reason you're here in town."

He gave a quick nod. "Of course. I was hoping to stop in there a bit today."

"It's a good time to go. Sundays are crafts days. Mr. Freider always has some kind of activity set up for the kids. I think it's gingerbread houses this time."

"Sounds fun. As long as it doesn't involve any baking," he quipped, then frowned as if realizing the lameness of the joke.

"I know Ray's been looking forward to it. We'll bring him with us. He should be up from his nap soon."

And he'd also make for a useful buffer between her and Justin, she added silently. They'd been in way too close proximity for the past several hours.

"Great idea."

Carli was right. By the time they got to Hammond's with Ray, the little boy had completely forgotten about the epic baking disaster and was back to his regular bouncy self. The prospect of decorating a gingerbread house proved an effective distraction.

If only Carli could find a distraction for herself. She was all too aware of Justin still. And all too quick to recall his kisses. Subconsciously, she ran a hand over her lips.

Stop it.

"This is a great crowd—" she made sure to point out "—despite the prospect of a major snowstorm that usually keeps people indoors."

"Point taken," Justin acknowledged.

She smiled with satisfaction. At least she had that much going for her, despite the circus that this visit was turning into.

Ray saw a little friend and immediately ran over to where the other child was setting up his craft area. He tugged Justin along with him.

"Hi, Josh," he said to the other boy, pronouncing the end of the name with a "th" sound. "This is my friend Justin," he added, and pointed up. "You know, like just in time."

Josh giggled and Ray looked pretty proud of himself. Justin crouched to both boys' level. He stuck out his hand.

"Nice to meet you, Josh. I'm a good friend of Ray here. You know, like ray of sunshine."

He said it with such a straight face that Carli had to laugh. Now both boys were giggling.

"Do another one," Ray demanded.

"Sure, ray-nee day."

The two boys collapsed on each other in a fit of giggles now.

"Your friend is funny," Josh proclaimed, and laughed some more. Justin was so naturally at ease with children. No wonder Ray had grown so fond of him in such a short time. Carli's eyes suddenly stung as she watched the three of them. It broke her heart that Justin had never been afforded the opportunity to be that carefree when he was little.

So different from the way she'd grown up. The Tynan girls had been pretty fortunate as children. Things were often crazy and hectic when you had four other siblings. It was a fact of life that things could get very competitive with five girls under one roof. Her younger twin sisters were constantly trying to better each other.

But she'd truly been blessed with a caring family unit and loving, doting parents. She couldn't deny that, no matter how betrayed she'd felt last year. Not only by Janie and Warren, but by the way her family had reacted in response. Carli tried not to bristle at those thoughts. She loved every last one of her family members, she really did. With all her heart. But not a single one of them had shared in her outrage. Not even Tammy. Essentially, they'd all just expected her to accept it and move on. For the sake of family harmony, no doubt. No one bothered to try to put her feelings first. The betrayal still stung, even after all these months.

"Hello. Earth to Carli. Come in, Carli." She looked up to find Justin waving a hand in front of her face.

"Sorry, I was just admiring all the kids' handiwork."

He nodded, then glanced around the store as the boys continued. He had to be noticing the numerous people in the aisles and line leading up to the checkout area. He had to see how well the store was doing. She just had to make him realize that it had the potential to be this way throughout the year. She knew Mr. Freider could pull it off. Carli would do whatever she could to help.

She turned to Justin to tell him so, but just right then he leaned over Ray to help him mount the base of his gingerbread house. Her nephew's smile widened with appreciation. And she knew no matter Justin's thoughts on the store, she was glad he was here with them.

Ray's gingerbread house was a complete failure. Between that and the baking fiasco earlier, Justin had to admit that he didn't possess a creative cell in his whole body. It didn't help that Ray kept popping the candy corn and gum drops into his mouth rather than using them as decorations.

"Your parents are here," Carli said to Ray, then took him by a sticky hand toward where Tammy and her husband, Raymond, had just walked in. Tammy gave her sister a hug. Her brother-in-law did as well, then turned to shake Justin's hand.

"Thanks for taking care of the little tyke," he said to them both. "We saw the cookies at the house. Decided to make mint ones this year, huh?"

Tammy laughed out loud, and Carli gave her a useless punch on the arm.

"What did I say?" her brother-in-law asked.

"Nothing. Never mind."

He shrugged and picked up his son. "Guess we'll see you all tomorrow then. Unless this storm has everybody housebound, that is. Looks like a nasty one."

Justin watched as the three of them left the store. Tammy hooked her arm inside her husband's as he carried their son. It was such a touching domestic scene. So simple. So pure.

For an insane moment, Justin thought about himself as part of such a picture. An image of him and Carli walking arm in arm the same way sprang into his head. He shook it away.

Hammond men didn't do the whole family thing. Look at what a fiasco it had been when his parents had tried.

"We should get going," Carli said, interrupting his thoughts. He was reaching for his coat when

Mr. Freider came rushing out to them. He held a framed photo in his hand.

"Wait. Justin, I have something for you." He held out the frame.

Justin reached for it, unsure what he was looking at. Then an unfamiliar sensation settled across his chest as he realized what it was.

"I don't understand."

"After you left yesterday, I remembered I had it. Thought you might want it as a memento."

"What is it?" Carli leaned over her arm to look.

"It's a newspaper clipping. Of a photo of me as a little boy." He held a toy truck in his hand, a big grin on his boyish face. He couldn't have been more than the age Ray was now.

Mr. Freider smiled. "That was the day of the store's grand opening. Your whole family came to cut the ribbon. This is from the write-up in the local paper."

Now that he studied the picture, Justin vaguely remembered the day. Even at that age, he could tell that his parents were simply going through the motions. But he and James had been excited nonetheless.

Unfortunately, the memory of it all had been

overshadowed by the stinging fight that occurred within hours of them getting home. No wonder he'd blocked it out.

Until now. Justin found his mouth had gone dry. "I don't know what to say, Mr. Freider. This is such a thoughtful gesture."

"Nonsense. We picked up several copies of that issue all those years ago. Of course, the paper it's printed on has yellowed a bit. But not bad for twenty something years, huh?"

"No." Justin choked out the word over an achy lump that had formed in his throat. "It's not bad at all. I can't thank you enough."

Mr. Freider's smile grew wider. "Like I said, it wasn't that big a deal. Just thought it might recall some happy memories."

But it was a big deal. Bigger than Mr. Freider would ever know. He tucked the picture under his arm and went to shake the older man's hand.

But Mr. Freider had other ideas. He embraced Justin in a big bear hug. "You two have a good night now. That snow's about to come down at any minute. Much earlier than they said."

"You, too, Mr. Freider."

Out on the sidewalk, Justin couldn't help but glance at the picture once more.

"You were a very cute child," Carli said.

"Think so?"

She pointed to the frame. "No doubt about it. Look at those big round eyes, the thick wavy hair. Very cute."

It was childish, but her words pleased him to a ridiculous degree. "That was very nice of him."

"Mmm-hmm," Carli agreed. "He's one of a kind."

So are you. The words hovered on his tongue but he knew not to speak them out loud.

"No one's ever done anything like that for me before."

Carli looked up and studied the air. "He also seems to have been right about the snow." A big fat snowflake landed on her nose. He had to clench his fist to keep from brushing it off with his finger. Then kissing the spot where it had landed.

There were plenty more to follow. Suddenly, a flurry of white flakes blew like confetti all around them.

By the time they reached the inn, the snow was

blinding. He couldn't believe the speed at which it fell, accompanied by a blinding cold wind he could feel down to his bones.

"Well, looks like you'll be snowed in at least for the night." Carli stopped in front of the glass door. "I'll call you later tomorrow. Make sure to charge your cell phone as soon as you get in. We're likely to lose power at some point." She turned to walk away. "I should be getting home."

He gently grabbed her by the arm. "There is no way I'm letting you walk back alone to your house." He could barely see her face in front of him for the white cloud of snow between them. "Not in this mess."

"I'll be fine," Carli assured him. But he wasn't buying it.

"No way," he insisted. "I'll come with you."

"And then what? You'd have to walk back here. And this is just going to get worse. Something tells me you won't be comfortable on my mom's lumpy couch all night if you get stranded there."

"I'll take my chances."

She looked ready to argue some more when Betty stepped outside. "What in the angel's name are you two doing out here? You'll both catch your death of a cold."

Without waiting for an answer, she physically ushered them both into the lobby. Carli looked ready to protest, but Betty stopped her with a no-nonsense look and thrust her hands on her hips.

"Carli Tynan. What kind of neighbor do you think I am? If l let you walk the rest of the way home in that?" She jutted her chin toward the window to indicate the snow.

"But Bet—"

"But nothing. I have plenty of extra rooms. You are staying here tonight. You can borrow something Leddy left here before heading away to college. And I don't want to hear another word about it. Now call your folks and let them know."

Another sleepless night. Despite all the homely comforts of the Sailor's Inn, Carli was getting no more rest tonight than she had the one before. The loud whooshing of the wind outside her window did not help the situation.

Sighing, she pulled off the covers and got out of bed. One more insomnia-laden night meant she was going to be a total wreck tomorrow.

Warm milk. It had never worked for her before, but it was worth a try. Betty wouldn't mind if she checked the kitchen fridge and heated some for herself. Things were getting desperate here.

The well-placed outlet night-lights afforded just enough illumination to make it downstairs without disrupting the other guests. There was at least one more couple staying at the inn. Within moments, she had a steamy hot cup of creamy milk in her hands. Not quite ready to go back upstairs, Carli made a detour through the lobby into the main sitting room. She'd always loved this room, even as a small child when her mother had come to visit Betty and dragged her girls along. Carli had spent hours sitting in front of the large fireplace with her book while her mother and Betty chatted over tea. She walked over to the hearth now. It was no longer a wood fireplace. The Mills had a newer, more convenient electronic model installed several years ago. But the rest of the room looked achingly familiar. Carli flipped the switch on the wall and a blue-tinged fire roared to life in front of her. She sighed with satisfaction as the heat spread over her skin.

"You can't sleep either, huh?"

Though he'd spoken softly, the unexpected sound of Justin's voice behind her made her jump. Warm milk sloshed over her cup and spilled onto her hand. She wiped it away on the side of her borrowed nightgown.

"Justin, you startled me."

"Sorry," he said, and made his way into the room. He came to stand next to her by the fire. "I thought I'd come down and watch the storm through the big bay window down here. It's something to behold. All this snow."

"We get at least one or two of these a year, and it never ceases to amaze me, the sheer magnitude of their power."

"It's beautiful, really. The entire town covered in sparkling white. Like an ivory blanket sprinkled with glitter."

She turned to look at him. "Wow. That was very poetic. We'll see how pretty you think it is when it's time to shovel tomorrow. And don't think my father won't ask you to. Guest or not."

He laughed, then surprised her by lowering himself to the floor and sitting cross-legged in front of the fire. "I have an electric fireplace too," he offered. "Back in my condo in Seattle."

Feeling awkward and rude at speaking down to him from her standing position, Carli felt no choice but to join him on the thick faux fur rug on the floor. "Yeah?"

"Yes. Funny though. It's not nearly as…cozy as this one is. It's designed to look like a pit. With fake charcoal and kindling. I like this one much better."

She wasn't sure what to say to that so she remained silent and took another sip of her milk. It wasn't doing a thing to make her sleepy, not that she had any hope of that with Justin sitting right next to her. He wore drawstring flannel pajama bottoms that somehow looked sexy on him. And a crisp white T-shirt that accented his solid chest and biceps. She could feel his warmth next to her along with the warmth of the fire in front of them, like a safe comfortable cocoon.

An empty yet easy silence settled between them. This was nice, Carli decided, allowing herself to relax into a peaceful lull. There were worse ways to sit through a storm than lounging in front of a fire watching the flames while listening to the sound of the wind.

So she wasn't prepared for what came next.

When he spoke again, the next words out of Justin's mouth shocked her to her core.

"I need to ask you something. Are you in love with your sister's boyfriend?"

Justin hadn't meant to blurt it out that way. Subtle, it was not. Carli was clearly uncomfortable now, and he could have kicked himself for that. They'd been having such a pleasant and casual conversation. He'd just ruined the whole relaxed ambience with one question.

"Why do you ask?" She took a sip from her mug, not taking her eyes off the fire.

They were sitting so close together, his knee brushed against hers when he turned. Shadows from the flames fell across her face and highlighted the silky chocolate brown of her eyes. He fought the urge to pull her into his lap.

"Never mind. Forget I said anything."

"But you did."

"I shouldn't have. It's none of my business. I apologize."

Carli set the cup she'd been holding on the floor. "There's nothing between Warren and me," she said with a firm note of finality.

She was clearly uncomfortable talking about it. Which had to mean there was something there. A surge of emotion shot through his chest, a feeling he refused to acknowledge as jealousy. What he'd said earlier was true. It really was none of his business. In a few short days, he'd be back on the West Coast and likely not see Carli Tynan again for a good long time, if ever. There could never be anything real between them. Carli wasn't the type to have a casual fling, and there was no way he could give her anything more.

"He and I had a messy breakup about a year ago. I was angry and betrayed when he ended it."

Justin sucked in a breath. Hearing how much she'd cared for another man affected him way more than he would have liked, more than it should have.

"Because you were in love with him."

"I thought I was. But he fell for my sister. As I'm sure you surmised at dinner."

"I can't imagine that." He meant that with all his heart. How could any man prefer the quiet, albeit beautiful sister to the dynamic, intelligent woman who sat beside him now?

She looked off into the fire, the reflection of the flames dancing in her eyes.

"Why do I get the feeling there's more to the story?" Justin prodded.

She didn't look away from the fire when she answered. "Very perceptive, Mr. Hammond."

"So I'm right."

"Yes. But the summary is that I felt betrayed and deceived. The two of them were too afraid to tell me what was happening at first. Maybe for fear of hurting me, I don't know. But I just felt deceived. To make matters worse, I felt like my parents sided with Janie, at first."

"How so?"

She shrugged. "Little things. Warren was still always welcome at the house. I know that sounds petty. But I felt like he should have been made to feel at least a little out of place." Her chest heaved as she took a deep sigh. "Plus, Mom and Dad would make these quaint remarks about how things that are meant to be will happen. Or not. You know, que será, será."

He wasn't sure what to say to that. After witnessing how close the family was, he couldn't imagine what it must have felt like to think you were losing your place within it.

She wrapped her arms around herself, lost in her thoughts. Justin had never felt a stronger urge to comfort someone. He leaned closer to her, literally giving her a shoulder to lean on if she so wanted.

It thrilled him beyond words when she took him up on the offer and placed her head gently against him.

He could smell the sweet fruity scent of her shampoo. Her warmth settled over his skin. "I have to tell you something," he began.

"Hmm?"

"I think Warren is a fool."

Her first response was to snuggle in closer to him. "But you've seen my sister."

"So?"

He could feel her breathing; her hair tickled his chin. "So she's stunningly beautiful. Poor Warren can hardly be blamed."

He cupped her chin, turning her face to his. "I'll repeat. Warren is a fool."

Carli sucked in a breath, studied his face. She

was so close, barely half an inch separated them. "Do you really think so?"

"Without a doubt. Janie's a pretty girl. But I never went for the frail, dainty type. I prefer women with unruly hair and inner strength. Like you."

She swallowed, and he couldn't resist leaning even closer. "You do?"

"Oh, yeah."

Justin didn't even know who moved first. He just thanked the heavens that suddenly her lips were on his. She tasted like sugar and cream, her mouth warm and soft against his. It was the slightest, gentlest of kisses.

But somehow he felt it through to his soul.

What time was it? Justin awoke disoriented and confused. The wind outside rattled the windows. There was a clear crisp chill in the air; the fireplace had gone out. The room was dark as hades. They must have lost power at some point, as Carli had predicted. But somehow he felt surprisingly warm. It took a moment for his eyes and senses to focus.

He realized with a shock why he wasn't cold.

Carli was nuzzled against him, cradled along his length. Her back snug tight against his stomach.

They'd fallen asleep in front of the fireplace. Right there on the faux fur rug. His traitorous body immediately reacted.

Control.

But it was no use. He was only human, and he'd been wildly attracted to this woman from the moment he'd laid eyes on her. His arousal hit fast and strong. She'd be horrified if she woke up and became aware of the current state he was in.

"Carli, wake up."

Her response was to nuzzle her head against the bottom of his chin. The action did nothing to diminish his arousal. He bit out a silent curse.

"Carli. Hon. It's the middle of the night."

That attempt didn't work either. She moaned softly and shifted closer to him. Justin couldn't help but groan out loud. This was torture. He dared a glance at her face. Thick dark lashes framed her closed lids. She looked so peaceful, so content.

He couldn't do it. He couldn't force her awake. Just a few more minutes. Let her get some rest, she'd been yawning all day yesterday. Clearly she needed the sleep.

He would just have to suffer it out for a while.

Justin found himself second-guessing that decision three hours later when he heard footsteps approaching. Through some miracle, he'd fallen asleep despite his inconvenient reaction to having Carli in his arms. And now someone was about to find them in a very compromising position.

There was nothing for it, nothing he could do to try to rectify the situation. Way too late for that.

Making himself look up, Justin found Betty staring down at them with clear shock on her face. But was there also a ghost of a smile? She cleared her throat. Loudly.

Carli awoke with a start and jolted back in his arms. A harsh flash of pain shot through his jaw as the top her head connected hard with his chin. He couldn't help his grunt in response.

"Good morning," Betty said, as if nothing was amiss.

Carli removed herself from his grasp. She

opened her mouth to speak and then promptly shut it again. Clearly at a loss for words, she sat up.

"Hello, Betty," Justin managed to choke out. His jaw actually clicked. Just then the lights flickered and the power came back on. Something hummed back to life in the kitchen area, and the fireplace lit up.

"Well, thank goodness," Betty said, still staring at the two of them. She had to be referring to the lights coming back on, right?

"Mr. Freider has been trying to get a hold of you, dear." She addressed Carli. "I'm afraid he has some bad news."

Justin helped Carli to her feet and then stood himself, ignoring the aches and pains that came with sleeping on a hard floor all night.

"What's happened?" Carli asked, a little unsteady on her feet.

"It's the toy store. Apparently, the roof was too weak for the massive onslaught of snow in such a short period of time. It collapsed under the weight, snapping a water pipe as it came down." She took a breath. "I'm afraid the store has flooded."

Carli gasped. "Oh, no. How much damage?"

"I'm sorry, dear. That's all I know."

CHAPTER ELEVEN

IT WAS EVEN worse than she'd feared. The whole back corner of Hammond's Toys Cape store looked like a demolition zone. Carli bit back a cry of despair as she and Justin entered what was left of the store. Most of the damage had occurred in her favorite section, the Book Nook. Her heart broke when she saw the collapsed shelves, the scattered books with soaked and torn pages. A mountain of snow had piled up in the corner; thick icicles covered the shelves.

Mr. Freider was already there, trying to save anything that was salvageable. The poor man must have been freezing. Either that, or he was shaking from sheer sadness. Probably both.

"Oh, Mr. Freider." She walked over and gave him a gentle hug. "We'll find a way to fix all this." Though she couldn't imagine how. The store's very existence was already in jeopardy. Not that Mr. Freider had any idea. And now this.

He gave her a skeptical look. "Thank you for coming, dear."

"Would you like me to call the insurance company?"

For some reason, Mr. Freider's eyes started to tear up at the question. Then she understood. Technically, this would be considered flood damage. Something most insurance companies didn't cover.

This was devastating. What were the chances Justin would ever commit to keeping the store open now? It would take considerable cost and resources to repair all this and open up again.

"The alarm went off and alerted me at home around dawn," Mr. Freider told them. "I ran down as soon as I could to shut the water off. But by then…" He let the sentence trail off. "For it to happen this time of year."

Justin stepped over and placed a hand on the other man's back. "Why don't you take a break, Mr. Freider. Go home for a couple of hours. If you've been here since dawn, you're past due for some rest.

"Carli and I will take over for a while," Justin added when he hesitated. Finally he gave a reluctant nod and put down the book he'd been holding.

Carli watched him walk away and had an urge to hug Justin too—for the consideration and kindness he'd just shown. "That was very thoughtful of you."

Justin shrugged. "He looked ready to collapse. It was a no-brainer to send him home."

"Where do we start?"

"I'm going to find some boxes. He must have some empty shipping boxes somewhere."

"What for?"

"We can't do this out here. We'll freeze. It'll be easier and more effective if we work in batches. We'll carry a box or two at a time to his office and sort them out there."

"Great idea." Good thing one of them was thinking straight. "I'm sure there's some empty boxes in the storage area. Follow me."

Twenty minutes later, Justin had covered the exposed area with a heavy tarp he'd found in the storage room and the two of them were in the back office. They'd already made several piles, sorting through the various books and items depending on their level of damage.

Despite the unfortunate distraction with the flood, Carli couldn't stop thinking about what had happened this morning. Or last night. Justin had to be thinking about it too. How could he not? They'd spent the night in each other's arms. The fact that it had happened without knowledge or intent mattered little. He'd been the perfect gentleman; she had to let him know how much that meant to her.

"Thank you for helping me with this." Carli clutched the book she was holding against her chest like a shield. "And there's something else I should thank you for."

"What's that?"

"Last night. When you...uh...you know... didn't even try. I mean, all we did was sleep." She clutched the book tighter. Why was this so hard?

"Trust me, it wasn't for lack of wanting to." He blew out a breath. "If you only knew."

Electricity cackled between them. "You shouldn't say such things."

Justin visibly stiffened. "What exactly am I supposed to say to that?" He threw the question out like a challenge, a hard glint in his voice. Anger flashed in his eyes.

"Is something bothering you?"

"One of my family's retail locations has just incurred considerable damage."

She nodded, mustered a wealth of sarcasm into her voice. "Mmm-hmm. You've cared so much about the family business over the years, I can see how that would agitate you now."

She saw immediately that it was the wrong thing to say. He clearly didn't appreciate the sarcastic remark. Justin's mouth tightened into a thin line. But she wasn't buying that his sour mood was the result of the flood or the damage it had caused. So what else could it be?

"You know what's bothering me?"

A shiver ran through Carli at his tone and the tightness in his shoulders. But she decided to take the bait. "What?"

Suddenly, he'd moved in front of her. A mere breath separated them. Her heart pounded in her chest. She couldn't even tell if it was due to the proximity or because of the frustration blaring in his eyes.

"The way you're standing there thanking me

for not touching you last night." With a finger, he lifted her chin. "When I make love to a woman, I can guarantee you it won't be when she's half asleep and tired after a restless night."

Her mouth went dry. She'd simply meant to thank him. "I didn't mean to imply otherwise." He had to know that.

"Right. I just have one question: Did you want me to?"

Well, he'd clearly gone and thrown the gauntlet down, hadn't he? She refused to lie. "I think you know the answer to that."

"Oh, no you don't. You're not getting off that easy. Answer the question. Did you want me to?"

Her breath caught in her throat. But she blurted out the only answer she could. "Yes."

She didn't know what she'd been expecting, but in the next instant, she found herself lifted up by the hips. Justin carried her the few steps to the desk behind them. Then he set her down and conquered her lips with a savage kiss.

Desire slammed through her as he ran his hands along her rib cage, then plunged them into her hair. She wanted him, all of him. The taste of him sent fire through her nerve endings, igniting wants and needs she could no longer hope to suppress. All that mattered was this moment and where it might lead to. She lay back on the desk surface, bringing him down with her. All the while, his hungry lips continued their sweet onslaught.

Something shifted under her weight and dug into the small of her back. The small nuisance was just distracting enough that Carli regained some semblance of sanity. On a regretful moan, she gave Justin a gentle push and he immediately pulled back. She straightened back to a sitting position.

"What the—" But Justin didn't finish. He appeared as shell-shocked as she felt.

Dear God, she'd nearly made love to him right there in the middle of the store office, on top of a metal desk. A man she hardly knew. What if someone had walked in? Or worse, what if one of her parents had come to the store to check on her? It was bad enough Betty had discovered them asleep in front of the fireplace this morning.

The thought of someone walking in on the two of them was too horrifying to further contemplate.

One thing she knew for certain. She'd become an unrecognizable version of herself since Justin Hammond had arrived in her life. She didn't like this incarnation of Carli. A woman who was too reckless and too unrestrained. It had to stop. All of it.

One way or another, they were going to have to resolve the question about the fate of the store. Then she was going to have to return to her previous life. And to her previous self.

Justin stepped away from Carli and rammed his hand through his hair. Damn it. What was it about her that made him lose control the way he did? He barely had a grasp on it now. She arranged her top and fixed the collar, breathing heavy all the while. Her lips were swollen from his kiss, her cheeks reddened from the stubble he had due to not having had time to shave this morning. He knew it was insane, but all he wanted to do was rub that stubble all over her soft, supple skin. Leave his mark on every inch of her body.

She may have done the sensible thing and pushed him away just now, but her eyes were clouded with passion and desire. For him. She wanted him as much as he wanted her.

But not here, not now.

The roar of a siren pulled them both out of a breathless stupor. The sound grew closer and within seconds could be heard right outside the wall. Damn it. He should have figured the fire marshal would want to come make sure the building was structurally sound.

"The fire department," he told Carli. Her clothes were in disarray, her hair a mess of tangles from the way he'd rammed his hands through her curls.

"I'll go greet them, if you want to…you know." He motioned to her.

"Yes, thank you. I'd like a minute or so."

Rubbing his chin in frustration and self-reproach, he left the office, the taste of her on his tongue still teasing his senses.

It took the fire marshal less than fifteen minutes to declare the building safe pending an electrician's assessment. Also, he told them that they'd been lucky to actually lose power as the flooding could have cause an electrical fire.

Justin saw the man off and went to tell Carli the news. His phone vibrated in his pocket before he got far. A text had arrived from Jackson. To call him as soon as he had a free moment.

Justin sighed. No time like the present.

He dialed the number and waited as Jackson answered.

"Mr. Freider called me," Jackson said. "How bad is the damage?"

"Pretty bad. It's going to take a huge amount of resources to restore and become operational again. My original conclusion makes even more sense now…" He paused, an idea suddenly occurring to him. "But if you're going to put money into restoration, it might be an opportunity to invest a bit more and take the unit into an expanded direction."

"I'd be very interested in hearing about that."

"I'll sum up the proposal and email it to you."

Justin ended the call and returned the cell phone to his pants pocket. He might have come up with a way to make the flood damage an opportunity in disguise.

Jackson sounded open to the idea. He had no doubt Carli would love it. He couldn't wait to tell her.

* * *

Justin had been gone for quite a while. Was the fire marshal taking that long to wrap things up?

Carli's curiosity got the better of her and she left the office to go find him. To her surprise, Justin was in the hallway speaking to someone on the phone. She immediately turned to give him some privacy until she heard a snippet of the conversation.

He was talking to Jackson.

"My original conclusion makes even more sense now..."

That was all Carli needed to hear. She felt like she had just taken a punch to the midsection.

Without her knowledge or her input, Justin was speaking to his father about the future of the store. And from the sound of it, he was making the argument that storm damage had only served to finalize his decision. He thought it should be shut down. She ran back into the office and slammed the door shut.

Justin had betrayed her.

He hadn't even bothered to mention anything to her before making his decision. He'd just gone straight to Jackson. Using the storm as an excuse to argue for what he'd originally planned all along.

Like a fool, she'd gone ahead and trusted yet another man she shouldn't have.

A knock sounded on the door. "Are you decent yet?" Justin asked from the other side.

With a huff of annoyance, Carli strode to the door and pulled it open to let him in.

Justin's smile faded from his lips when he saw the look on her face.

"Has the wrecking crew been called in then?" she demanded to know.

He blinked at her. "I beg your pardon."

"I suppose we'll need to auction or donate the remaining items."

"I'm afraid I still don't understand."

"You were talking to Jackson just now, weren't you?"

"Yes, I called him after—"

She cut him off with a dismissive wave of her hand. Her heart sank further. So Justin *had* been the one to initiate the phone call.

"I know why you called him. And you did it behind my back."

"What are you talking about?"

"You didn't have to courtesy to come to me first. Just went ahead and gave your decision to your father. I don't expect someone like you to understand just how wrong that was."

"Someone like me?"

"You've never felt a loyalty to anyone or anything, have you? That's why you don't give a damn about keeping this store open. You never felt the sense of belonging that a place like this affords to the people who love it. After all, you never really felt like you belonged or were a part of anything, did you? Not to a town. Not to a family. All you manage to do is ruin things for others."

"Wait just a minute—"

She didn't want to hear it. Not right now. She had no use for his explanation, which that would no doubt involve numbers and returns and all the factual things that men like him always cared so much about. She crossed her arms in front of her chest to quell the shaking that had suddenly gripped her and turned away. "Just go."

Justin had heard enough. Carli's anger was palpable. And why? All because he'd had the nerve to talk to Jackson without her knowledge. She didn't even care what the content of the conversation may have been. Her immediate assumption had been to think the worst.

You never really belonged...

Well, he had better things to do with his time than to try to explain himself to her.

He stepped closer to where she stood. Even now, with her anger directed straight at him, he couldn't help but long to pull her to him, to kiss her fury away until they both couldn't care less about some damn store and some ruined toys.

He clenched his fists at his side instead.

She paced around the desk, then turned to shoot him an accusatory look. A wealth of anger shone in her eyes. All directed at him.

Something snapped within his soul as he met her gaze. Somehow, some way, he'd done it again. He'd damaged something precious. Damned if he knew how or why. But it seemed to be a talent he had.

Served him right for ever thinking things could be any different. And curse Carli Tynan for ever leading him toward that misconception in the first place.

Well, he'd heard enough. "I'm not sure why you're so worked up. But understand this—I don't need to run my intentions by you or anyone else."

She gasped, then lifted her chin. "You're absolutely right. I'm not sure why I thought you would have the decency to do so."

Justin didn't bother to reply to that. Without a word, he turned and stepped out of the office.

After all, what was there left to say?

Justin walked out of the rental agency and over to the late model SUV he'd just secured. He'd drive back to Boston, then arrange for a flight out of Logan. There was nothing left for him to do here.

In the interest of professionalism, he'd stop by Hammond's corporate office building and give his father a quick summary. Not that it mattered at this point.

Shame too. He actually may have figured out a way to save Carli's precious store and make some money for Hammond's in the process. Well, it was none of his concern now.

Getting into the rental vehicle, he started the ignition, then sighed and pounded the steering wheel with his fist. Damn it. None of this felt right.

Every inch of him wanted to delay leaving, despite what had just happened back at the store. Only one explanation for it.

There was no denying he had inexplicably, unwittingly developed deeply serious feelings for Carli Tynan.

Look where it had led. He didn't have it in him to have a healthy relationship. Certainly not with a woman like Carli who had a rich, fulfilling life. With family and friends who loved her.

Look how much havoc he'd caused her in the short time he'd known her.

Had it really been barely a week since he'd touched down at Logan Airport for the first time? It felt like years had gone by. The fact was, he'd be leaving a changed man. More so than he would have ever guessed.

He should have never come to New England. He'd known it was a bad idea from the beginning to come here, running to do Jackson's bidding like an eager errand boy. He should have known it wouldn't end well.

The conversation with Betty Mills had been

awkward and uncomfortable when he'd gone to grab his belongings from the inn. She didn't buy the explanation that he had to leave early due to a pressing business matter back in his Seattle office. The woman was too perceptive by half. She'd told him to visit again as soon as he could. He assured her he would. A lie. Betty would most likely never see him again, as sad as that was.

He didn't have any business here in Westerson, regardless of how fond he'd grown of everyone he'd met during his short stay.

Now, sitting in the driver's seat of the rental, all he wanted to do was drive straight out of town and keep going until he reached Logan Airport.

Begrudgingly, he realized he couldn't do that. It would be a coward's way out. He had to at least talk to Carli like a man and tell her he was leaving. And somehow explain that he hadn't intended to mislead her in any way.

Not the easiest conversation.

He shifted into gear. Best to just get it over with. If he was lucky, Ray would be there at the house. He didn't want to leave without saying goodbye to the little guy. Justin realized with a start that he would genuinely miss him.

Carli was on the porch as he approached the driveway. Unfortunately, she wasn't alone.

Justin swore out loud. He just wanted to talk to her one-on-one, in private, to say all the things that needed to be said between them. For one final time. Unfortunately, it appeared that waiting for her to finish with whoever she was with was his only option. The last thing he wanted was a delay right now. He started to pull over across the street. After all, she wouldn't recognize the car.

But then he realized three of her sisters and her mother were surrounding her. They were all laughing, sharing snacks and a bottle of wine. The scene was the perfect picture of a close, tight-knit family. A family full of love and affection. It was a picture someone like him had no business interrupting. Or trying to be a part of. Not with his history.

Her angry words echoed in his head once more—*I don't expect someone like you to understand.*

An image of the Christmas tree crashing down in the Hammond foyer flashed across his vision. No, there was really no point in talking to Carli.

Justin drove on.

CHAPTER TWELVE

JUSTIN RODE UP the elevator to the top floor of the Hammond corporate office building. Still late afternoon. If he knew his father, the old man would still be at his desk.

He didn't intend to be here long. He wasn't going to leave Boston without personally notifying his father that as far as he was concerned, his responsibilities here were finished. Justin would email him the figures and ideas at a later time. Not that it mattered at this point. But the professional businessman in him wouldn't let it slide. Not even when it came to his father.

To his dismay, Jackson's office was empty. The lights turned off. Justin bit out a curse. He probably should have called first, but he'd been certain Jackson would still be at work.

"Justin? Can I help you?"

He turned to find Miranda, his old babysitter,

in the hallway. "I was just looking for Jackson. Is he traveling?"

"No, dear. Believe it or not he's already gone for the day."

He had to admit he wasn't quite sure if he believed it. At his curious stare, Miranda gave a small shrug. "He's a different man these days. Ever since the Fryberg acquisition. Frankly, both your father and brother are behaving out of the norm."

Could nothing go his way today? He really didn't need to go back to that house. The Hammond mansion held no fond memories for him. "They have?"

She nodded. "No one can figure out why, but Jackson's been leaving earlier and earlier. Some days he calls to say he's working from home."

Justin didn't even know what to say to that. This was his father they were talking about, right? The same man he didn't see for days at times as a child because he came home late from work and left early the next day?

"Anyway, is there something I can help you with?" Miranda asked.

"No, thank you."

"Okay then." She turned to go, but Justin felt an uncharacteristic tug in his chest. He hadn't had a chance to say goodbye to anyone besides Betty back in Westerson.

And he had no idea if he would ever see Miranda again, for that matter. It surprised him that he cared. "Wait."

"Yes, dear?"

"I just want to say how glad I am that I got to see you again, after all these years. I'm leaving tonight. So I guess this will have to be goodbye." The words left his mouth in a swift torrent. He wasn't used to being so damn sentimental. What had Carli Tynan done to him? With some awkwardness, he extended his arm to shake Miranda's hand.

She ignored it and wrapped him in a big bear hug instead. He gingerly hugged her back. "Do you have to leave so soon?" she asked against when she finally let him go.

"I'm afraid so. I just need to wrap some things up with my father, and then I need to be on my way."

"I see. It's a shame James missed you entirely. I think it would have been good to have you two see each other again." She slammed a hand against her chest. "Silly me. Just look at me sticking my nose where it doesn't belong. But it broke my heart to see you boys yanked apart all those years ago. I think about it a lot."

"You do?"

"Of course. It was wrong. So wrong. James just wasn't himself those first few years after."

"He wasn't?"

She studied him with wide eyes. "Of course not. I know you must have struggled too, dear. But I saw firsthand how hard it was for that little boy to have his mother and brother just disappear like that."

Justin had to admit, with no small amount of shame, that he hadn't really given James much thought over the years. After all, he'd been the son who'd gotten to stay home, able to grow up in the same house he was born in. He slept in the same bed, kept attending the same school.

Whereas Justin's whole life had been upended.

But of course, it couldn't have been easy for James either. Justin hadn't allowed himself to think about that. The reason was simple really: he knew James blamed him for all of it.

And he wasn't wrong to do so.

"I wondered a lot about how you were doing," Miranda added. "But I never doubted you'd grow to be a successful, decent young man."

Justin had to stifle a groan. A decent man would have tried harder to get Carli to understand. Instead he'd simply walked off. But she'd get over it, he was sure. Judging by what he'd seen on the porch, maybe she had already started to.

"I wish I could have watched you grow up," Miranda added, breaking into his thoughts. Tears shimmered in her bright blue eyes, which had grown dimmer and surrounded by more wrinkles over the years. This woman had genuinely cared for him. He'd been too much of a child to appreciate that at the time. The notion brought on a profound sadness. It might have made a difference all those years ago if he'd only known there was someone he could have turned to.

"Thank you. But I guess that ship sailed when my father made his choice."

"Your mother did the leaving, dear. She took you with her."

Justin had to laugh at that. Why was he getting

into all this anyway? With a woman he barely remembered. Simply because she'd watched him a few evenings when he was a child. "Maybe so. But my father didn't exactly go out of his way to reach out me. No, he chose the son he wanted to keep with him just as much as my mother did."

Miranda patted his cheek. "But don't you see?"

"See what?"

"From where James stood, it was the exact same thing. As far as he was concerned, you were the favored one."

"I don't understand."

"Your mother chose you. And she never looked back. He was the one who was left behind."

With her words, Justin had to face a possibility he'd never let himself entertain before. His brother hadn't fared any better in the aftermath of their parents' breakup.

All these years, he and James had lived alternate versions of the same reality. Their lives were just flip sides of the same coin.

Where was Justin now? She hadn't heard from him, only knew that he'd left yesterday per Betty. Carli needed to get going too. This morning, the contractors had started reparations on the store. All that was left to do was to grab her bag and drive back to Boston. So why was she putting off the inevitable?

She glanced at her phone for the thousandth time, trying to decide whether to call him or not. He shouldn't have gone behind her back as he did. But throwing his lack of family in his face was clearly a low blow. Something she wasn't exactly proud of now upon reflection.

Carli swore out loud and threw her cell phone across her parents' living room. Luckily, it landed on the couch.

"Annoying spam?" A delicate voice startled her. She turned to see Janie standing in the doorway.

Carli squeezed her eyes in frustration. "I'm trying to decide if I should call Justin. I might owe him an apology."

"Oh?"

"Yeah… I may have said some things I shouldn't have."

"Then I think you should just bite the bullet and call. He might be waiting for you," Janie offered.

Carli blew out a puff of air in frustration. "More

likely, he never wants to talk to me again. He couldn't wait to get out of town."

Janie nodded. "Yeah, Mom may have mentioned something about him leaving prematurely."

"Thanks to me."

"Wanna talk about it?"

The question caught Carli off guard. The truth was, Janie was the first person she'd always been able to talk to. That was part of the reason this whole past year had been so hellish. She'd lost a dear confidante when things had turned icy between them. All those times Carli had thought to reach out but had been too stubborn to do so. And for what? A relationship with a man who she'd never really believed would work out anyway.

"I made a huge mistake," Carli admitted on a low sob, not even certain if she was still referring to Justin or the wedge that had been sitting between her and Janie for the past year.

Janie rushed over to her. Soon they were both holding each other as the tears flowed like a sudden rain. "Me too, sis. Me too," Janie said, then handed her a tissue from the side table and grabbed one for herself.

"Are we okay?" Janie asked, dabbing her eyes. "Please say yes."

"We will be," Carli answered, realizing she'd known that all along. "But I just wish you'd told me. When it first started between you and Warren."

Janie nodded. "You're right. It was just so hard. Neither one of us wanted to hurt you. That was the only reason we kept it from you at the beginning. You have to believe that."

Carli gulped back a sob.

"I've missed you," Janie said, her voice a scratchy rasp from her crying.

"I've missed you too."

If only one of them had had the courage to admit that before so much time had passed. She wouldn't have had to do without her closest sister for all these months. Not to mention, maybe she would never have lashed out at Justin the way she had after the storm.

She'd felt let down and betrayed when he'd called his father. Just as she'd felt betrayed by Janie and Warren. And her response at the first sign of trouble had been to put the blame squarely on Justin's shoulders, exactly the way his parents had when he was just a mere child.

She had to make this right.

"I think you have a phone call to make," Janie stated. "I'll give you some privacy."

"Thanks, sis."

Janie gave her a tight hug and left the room.

Carli didn't give herself time to think. Grabbing her phone, she clicked on Justin's number. But his phone went straight to voice mail.

A lump formed at the base of her throat. With her luck, Justin might very well be on a plane back to Seattle.

She was probably too late.

Carli rubbed her thumb absentmindedly along the corner of her mother's granite counter where a stubborn green stain still marked it. In time it would fade. She hoped so anyway. There were a lot of things she was banking on having time fix.

Though none of the mountains of snow had melted, the late-morning sunshine brought with it a golden touch to the vast amount of white outside. Everyone had shoveled out for the most part. Life in town was back to normal. But it felt anything but for her. She felt like the world had somehow tilted on its axis. Nothing would ever be the same.

Her mother walked in carrying a load of freshly laundered kitchen towels. It occurred to Carli how content her mother was, how so very in tune with her existence. Louise had worked hard all her life to build a loving home and a strong family, foundations that Carli had depended on growing up.

Alas, it appeared very unlikely that Carli would ever be able to achieve the same for herself. Not at the rate she was going when it came to men.

Her mom did a bit of a double take when she saw her. "I thought you'd be on your way by now. I heard Justin already left."

"He did indeed."

Her mother put the towels down and studied her with concerned, motherly eyes.

"I'm surprised you haven't. You usually can't wait to scram out of here and head back to the big city after a couple of days of visiting."

That was Louise, her mother was always straight to the point.

"Are you trying to get rid of me, Mom?" Carli

said with as much comical outrage as she could muster.

"Of course not." Louise came over and gave her small kiss on the top of her head. "But if you stick around, I'm very likely to put you to work. The pine needles that keep shedding off the Christmas tree and onto the floor need to be swept up. And heaven knows there's always more shoveling and deicing to do."

Carli held her hands up in mock surrender. "Okay. Okay. I was just leaving." But she didn't make a move out of her chair. "Can I just ask you something first?"

Louise's eyes narrowed; whatever she saw on Carli's face made her pull out a counter stool and sit across from her daughter.

"Shoot."

"It's about you and Dad."

Her mom lifted a finely shaped, dark eyebrow. "What about us?"

"You're just so, I don't know, strong together."

"I suppose. We've been together for over three decades."

"And then there's Tammy and Raymond. They're

just so happy together with their new house and their son."

"They were high school sweethearts. They've known each other a long time too."

"I know." She sighed deeply before continuing. "And now Warren and Janie."

Her mother leaned over and gave her hand an affectionate pat.

"Janie and I just had a bit of a chat," Carli told her. "Finally."

"Are you okay?"

Surprisingly, she was. Despite the shattered mass that now sat where her heart used to be, she genuinely felt no loss over Warren. Not anymore. "We are, Mom. I'm happy for them. I really am. I realize now they fit much better than Warren and I ever could."

"You may not have seen it at the time, but he wasn't right for you. You're too independent, too driven." She leaned closer before continuing. "He's the type who wants to stay in Westerson and plant more roots here. Just like Janie. You have to see now that those two belong together."

Carli sighed. "I do see that. Now. So do Tammy and Raymond. But you and Dad especially. I've seen you have arguments, but they never last. And you're both always so in tune." She took a deep breath; she had her mother's full attention now.

"Trust me when I tell you that wasn't always the case. None of you kids know this, but we almost broke off the engagement a month before the wedding."

Carli felt genuine surprise at that last comment. "You did? Why?"

"I was starting to get cold feet. And your father could tell. He didn't want to rush me into a commitment as serious as marriage if I wasn't totally ready for it."

"You? You were the one who got cold feet?"

"Believe it or not, there was a time I couldn't decide what I wanted or what path I needed to take in life to be happy. And your father was man enough not to put any pressure on me."

"Huh? I never knew."

"It's true. Now, every time I walk through this house, or hold my grandson—or even sit in the kitchen having a conversation with one of my girls—I know I made the right decision."

Carli felt the tears spring into her eyes. She

was so lucky to be part of this family, to be this woman's daughter.

So what if her love life was in shambles. In a few years, she may even be able to get over the foolish way she'd fallen for a man who had turned and walked out of her life at the first sign of discord.

"Tell me," her mother began. "Do your questions have anything to do with Justin Hammond perhaps?"

Carli wasn't surprised by the question. Louise Tynan was very on top of things when it came to her children. It was one of the reasons she loved her parents so much.

"As well as the way you were looking at him?" her mother added when she didn't respond right away.

Carli bit down on a bitter chortle. "I guess. But it's over. Almost as soon as it began."

"What happened?"

"I let my guard down. I wasn't careful enough and didn't see the obvious. Kind of like with Warren." She gulped down on a low sob. "But this feels so much worse, Mom. This feels like the hurt might never end."

Her mother stood and gathered her in her arms. "You've fallen for him."

"I'm afraid so."

"And he's leaving?"

"Probably flying out at this very moment."

"I see." She rubbed Carli's cheek. "Do you know why Dad and I mostly stayed out of the whole situation between you, Warren and your sister?"

She sniffled. "Because you wanted us all to learn a valuable lesson on how thoroughly Carli could make a fool of herself?"

Louise gave her an affectionate smile. "Hardly. Because we knew you would figure out what was best for you. You've always been good at deciding what you want and going after it."

"I am?"

"Indeed." She gave her arm a tender squeeze. "From what I can see, you've determined what you want. Now are you going to go after it?"

Justin had decided to sleep in for the first time in his life. But whoever was calling his cell phone apparently had other plans. The screen read Hammond Ent, so he picked it up without delay fully expecting Carli to be on the other end.

Only it wasn't Carli calling.

A bolt of disappointment shot through him. Foolish, wishful thinking. Carli wanted nothing to do with him. He'd managed to earn her ire and scorn. Just as he'd earned his brother's all those years ago when his antics had finally pulled the family apart.

No, the deep baritone voice on the other end of the line belonged to his father. Looked like he had indeed blown his chance to rectify things with her. Justin sat up in bed and rubbed the sleep out of his eyes.

"Do you have a moment, son?"

Would he ever get used to hearing that word coming from Jackson? He glanced at the bedside clock on the bureau across his hotel room: 8:30 a.m. Much later than he usually slept, but he'd been restless and unable to fall asleep last night, reliving the events of the previous day repeatedly in his head.

"Sure." He just had to wake up fully first.

"I wanted to let you know I was very impressed with the initial plans you sent over. Once the repairs to the Cape store are completed, I'd like to begin implementing your ideas."

Justin sighed with relief. He'd been fully prepared to take matters into his own hands if he had to. "I'm glad to hear it. I'm sure Carli will be more than anxious to get started on it all."

His father was silent a moment on the other end. "That's one of the things I'd like to discuss with you, in fact. I don't know what your plans are, but would you be able to come in later this morning to go over some of this?"

He couldn't mean what Justin was beginning to suspect he meant. Did he honestly have someone else besides Carli in mind to run the project? Rubbing his eyes, he answered, "I can be there within the hour."

"That's great, son. I'll see you then."

"Wait, Jackson."

"What is it?"

"I just want to be clear. All those ideas I proposed, I had Carli firmly in mind as the project manager to carry them through. I think she's the best qualified given how well she knows the store and the town."

He could hear his father's pride in Carli when he answered. "I couldn't agree with you more."

Then what was this all about?

Jackson gave him a jolt when he answered the unasked question. "I believe she may need some help. I wanted to talk to you about perhaps clearing your calendar for the next several months. Perhaps even permanently, depending on what you're comfortable with."

Now he was awake. "Never mind what I said earlier. I can be there in half an hour."

It took only twenty minutes.

His father was standing in front of his office window, staring down at the traffic bottleneck along Boylston Street when Justin knocked on his door.

Jackson motioned to the chair in front of his classic executive desk, and then waited for Justin to sit down before taking his own seat.

"Thank you for coming in so quickly, son."

"I had nothing else to do. What's this about?"

"To put it mildly, I'd like you to come back. Back to the Boston area, the Cape specifically.

Back as a Hammond working for Hammond's Toys."

Mildly? Justin would not have called that mild. Bluntly sharp was more like it. "Just like that?"

"I realize what it would mean. You have a life back in Seattle, but we can talk about relocation incentives."

Justin was too shocked to speak.

"You're a rightful heir of this company. You need to be here at the helm, along with your brother."

A jarring thought occurred to him. "Are you dying?"

Jackson's immediate response was a loud snort of laughter. "Not that I know of!"

"Then what's going on?"

"I've been doing some thinking. About both you and James. Your brother came to me before the holidays. Started a conversation we probably should have had years, perhaps even decades, ago."

Justin rubbed a hand down his face. If this was Jackson's attempt at some sort of reconciliation after all these years, he was totally unprepared for it.

"It made me realize how much I missed of you boys growing up. You especially."

Whoa. He definitely hadn't seen that coming. "I don't know what to say."

"Then I'll just do the talking for a bit." He took a deep breath as if to steady himself. "I know I should have tried harder to contact you. But your mother was a…a difficult woman. The time to cast blame or bad-mouth anyone is long gone. But she loved to remind me how much trouble you were."

"I remember."

"Only, you really weren't. I think you were a convenient way to prove to me that I was insufficient, that there was something I couldn't handle. I'm convinced she took you with her that night just to drive that point home. I couldn't handle you. So she left and took you with her."

Justin tried to process all he was being told. Given what he knew of his mother, it wasn't a terribly farfetched theory. But the idea that he'd simply been a pawn in his mother's argument stung more than he would have liked.

"That still doesn't explain why you chose to let her get away with it. Why you didn't make any kind of attempt to have some sort of contact, or even a relationship."

"I have no excuse, I'm afraid. Except that maybe on some level, I let her convince me of it too."

Jackson looked away then, studied a Bruins banner he had hanging on the wall to his left. "I know I should have tried harder to track you down. But she moved around so often. Support payments went direct to her bank account. And as the years grew longer, the prospect seemed more and more futile. But I'm trying now, if it's not too late."

A week ago, Justin would have told his father precisely that it was too late. But a lot had changed since then.

He'd met Carli Tynan.

Justin braced himself against the cold wind as he stood outside Carli's door on the footstep. He'd gone over various ways he might approach the conversation countless times in his head. But for the life of him, he still had no idea where he would start once she opened the door. He'd called earlier to tell her he would be stopping

263

by. To say she was shocked would be an under-statement. It had been unclear whether that was pleasant shock or the opposite. He supposed he was about to find out.

Taking a deep breath, he rang the doorbell, then waited. It opened within seconds and Carli stepped aside to let him. The apartment was just as festive as he remembered; Christmas decorations still adorned every wall and corner. Hard to believe that had only been a few short days ago.

"I'm surprised you're still in town." She looked different, tired. Dark smudges framed her eyes; her skin appeared paler. When she turned and walked to the sofa, there was unmistakably less of a spring in her step.

He had done that to her; he couldn't deny it. And he wanted to kick himself for his behavior. Well, it was the reason he was here.

"I decided to delay my return flight."

"I see. Can I get you anything? Coffee or something?"

This felt so wrong. Just a couple of days ago they'd spent the night sleeping in each other's arms in front of a cozy fireplace as a turbulent snowstorm raged outside. Now they were addressing each other as strangers.

"No, thank you."

She motioned to the loveseat he stood next to. "Have a seat."

He took off his coat and sat, trying once again to come up with the right words to say. He should have tried harder to make her understand at the store. Instead, he'd run.

Something he deeply regretted now.

He had to tell her that. But when he tried, they both started talking at the same time, awkwardly speaking over each other.

Justin ran a hand through his hair. "Please, go ahead."

"I was just wondering why you delayed your flight."

"Or why I'm here, for that matter?"

"That thought had crossed my mind, as well." She pulled her feet under her and positioned herself into a ball on the couch. "I imagine it has to do with the Cape store?"

"In part."

"I don't understand."

"I was actually just hoping to try to clear the air between the two of us."

"I see."

"I should have had the courtesy of listening to you that day, Carli."

Her gaze shifted downward, and she hugged her knees.

"I mentioned something to you the first day I arrived. When I made the mistake of judging you, do you remember that?"

"I think so, something about how it had nothing to do with me and everything to do with Jackson."

Bingo.

He should have known she was sharp enough to recall exactly what he was referring to. She was one of a kind. What a fool he was, to have had a chance with someone like her and to have blown it the way he had.

"And apparently, I didn't learn my lesson the first time I messed up."

Women like Carli didn't come along twice in one lifetime. His mishandling of it all was just one more thing in a long line of missteps he was going to have to live with. He got the distinct impression it might be the biggest. He had only himself to blame.

To spare her the effort of summoning a response, he stood and grabbed his coat. "I should leave. Thanks for giving me a minute."

Carli jumped up too. "Wait, before you go." She walked over to the oak angled desk under the corner window and pulled out a sketch pad. Tearing off the top sheet, she handed it to him. "I just finished it."

It took Justin a moment to realize what he was looking at. Then he remembered the framed sketch he had seen mounted along her parents' hallway.

She had drawn *him*. The piece of paper had one large portrait of him as an adult in the center and then another drawn smaller in the corner. The smaller one portrayed him as a boy. She had clearly based it on the newspaper captioned photo Mr. Freider had given him back at the Cape.

The resemblance in both was amazing, detailed and nuanced.

But more than merely replicating his physical features, the charcoal portrait seemed to capture his aura, right down to his soul. Only someone who had looked beneath the surface to his very core could have been able to draw him the way she had. The effect rendered him speechless.

"Do you like it?" she asked in a nervous and hesitant voice. How could she possibly be insecure with talent like that?

"It's the nicest thing anyone's ever given me. Or done for me, actually."

Yeah, he thought as he stared at the picture. He had definitely blown it.

CHAPTER THIRTEEN

CARLI HAD FULLY intended to give Justin the sketch since the moment she'd started it after the heartfelt conversation with her mother. It just hadn't occurred to her that he would be there in person to accept it. She'd expected to have to mail it to him at some point. When they were both somehow past the fateful events of the last week.

She figured that would have put the ball squarely in his court. He'd beaten her to the punch, however, when he'd surprised her with a phone call earlier this afternoon.

"I planned on rolling it and packaging it for you," she told him. "But since you're here, it's yours to take."

He blew out a deep breath. "I don't know what to say. Except I thought you said you had stopped sketching?" His gaze never left the paper he held in his hands.

"Yeah. I had. But I was inspired." She wasn't going to tell him just how inspired she'd been. The sketch had taken hours, and she'd been working nearly nonstop. In fact, she'd been tidying up furiously after receiving Justin's call that he was coming by.

It had been shocking enough to discover he was still in town. But to have him actually want to visit her apartment was a whole other level of altered reality. She wasn't entirely sure she wasn't dreaming this whole thing up at this very moment.

"I can't help but feel honored," he admitted, and a silly rush of girlish pleasure shot clear through her toes. "Can I ask you something?"

"Sure."

"Why did you ever stop in the first place? You have an amazing gift for it."

She had a hunch the question may have been coming. This was the risk she'd known she was taking when she picked up the charcoal pencil.

"Let me guess, it's a long story."

"Actually, it's not. It's quite an old, regular story, in fact."

He quirked an eyebrow in question.

"It's hard to put your heart into a drawing unless you feel a true joy in doing so. I'd lost that for a while. Now it seems to be back."

Justin's eyes flicked over her face. "I must say I'm honored."

She wanted to tell him there was so much behind her rendering of his image. His face was the first thing she saw when she closed her eyes before going to sleep. Those hazel eyes of his haunted her dreams and even her waking moment. But what purpose would it serve? Some things were better left unsaid.

She followed Justin as he made his way to the door. Suddenly, he pivoted on his heel. Carli's heart thud against her chest. He couldn't leave just yet.

"I almost forgot. I emailed you a document with detailing some ideas. For the Cape store. Please take a look when you get a chance."

Just a request to look at a file. "Oh, I'll be sure to do that."

Without another word, he opened the door and left.

Carli stared helplessly outside her window as she watched Justin walk briskly down the street, the sketch tucked under his arm. She felt torn and helpless. But what was there to do? They'd made their peace as best as could be expected.

So why did she feel like a boulder was sitting on her rib cage?

Just to give herself something to do, she flipped open her tablet and called up the email program. As he'd said, Justin's email sat toward the top. Clicking it open, she began to read.

It didn't take much time to come to a decision. She couldn't let Justin fly to Seattle and walk out of her life. She didn't even bother to grab her coat.

"Justin wait!"

Justin was almost afraid to turn around. What if he was simply imagining her voice? It was very likely he wanted to see her so badly that his mind was playing tricks on him. But when he turned around, there she was. Without a coat.

"Carli?"

He quickly went over to her; she was shivering. "You're freezing. And I don't even have a scarf to offer this time."

She laughed at that even as she rubbed her upper arms with her hands in an effort to get warm.

Justin didn't think about right or wrong at that moment. He simply went to her and put his arms around her shoulders, pulled her close.

"What are you doing out here? It's about twenty degrees."

Her teeth chattered as she answered him. "I think it's less than that."

He pulled her closer.

"I wanted to tell you I looked at the email," she said against the base of his neck.

"Okay. You could have simply typed a reply."

She shook her head. "No, that would not have worked."

"It wouldn't have?"

"No way. We clearly have to discuss all your suggestions in person."

A heady feeling of warmth began to spread through his chest. "I see."

With her in his embrace, he inhaled the scent of coconut shampoo and that soft subtle scent of hers that he'd grown so fond of. God, he'd missed it.

"There's no other way," she said, snuggled tight

up against him. "You're going to have to have dinner with me."

"Is that so?" he asked, unable to stop himself from dropping a hint of a kiss to the top of her head.

"Uh-huh. You're just lucky my mother passed on her lasagna recipe to all her girls."

She had no idea. Justin hadn't realized he could be so lucky. Lifting her chin with his finger, he decided he needed to show her with a kiss.

How in the world had he been talked into this? Justin adjusted the scratchy fake beard and groaned as he looked in the mirror in his new room at the Sailor's Inn. The answer stood next to him. Carli Tynan could probably get him to do anything with that sweet smile of hers.

Also, she'd reminded him of all the times he'd uttered the words "I'll make it up to you, somehow" since he'd met her. But this was hardly playing fair.

She stepped up to him and placed the velvet red hat atop his head. "You know, for someone who insists he's not really that into Christmas, you make a pretty good Santa Claus."

"If you say so." The goose-down pillow that was supposed to be his fake stomach threatened to drop once more, and he tightened the belt that held it up. Carli had informed him this morning that the actor who usually played Santa at the Westerson snowman competition had backed out due to a nasty case of the flu. She thought Justin would be the perfect replacement as he was the stranger in town and therefore less likely to be recognized by the older children.

Frankly, he didn't think he was going to be able to fool anybody. For one thing, every time he tried to yell "Ho-ho-ho!" he sounded utterly ridiculous. Which was exactly how he felt.

"You'll do fine," Carli reassured him. "You just have to walk around the tree farm commenting on all the contestant snowmen and hand out a few toys along the way. Hammond's was very sweet to donate those, by the way. Not to mention the matching donation to Toys for Tykes."

He shrugged. "I'm surprised there wasn't any kind of donation program to that charity up until now."

"There wasn't one until you started it." She gave him a peck on the cheek.

"Uh-uh." He grabbed her gently by the waist, pulling her up against his length. "You're gonna have to do better than that. Seeing as you're the only reason I'm dressed in this ridiculous costume and about to make a complete fool of myself."

Taking him up on his challenge, Carli hooked her arms around his neck and brought his mouth down to hers.

"How's that?" she asked with a breathless sigh when he finally managed to pull away.

"I'd say it'll do. For now."

The truth was he'd never be able to get enough of her. They'd been spending most of the days together since that fateful morning he'd stopped by her apartment. To think he had almost simply emailed her then left town. Taking the chance to go see her had been the best decision he'd ever made.

Unlike the decision to agree to this whole Santa thing. That was a totally different story. Carli noted the time on her cell phone. "We should make our way down. It's officially about to start. We'll have to sneak you out the inn's receiving door in the back of the building."

"Just tell me I don't have to ride in a sled."

The tree farm was bustling with activity when they arrived. Justin hoisted the toy bag over his shoulder and was immediately surrounded by a slew of youngsters.

"Santa's here!"

Despite himself, Justin had to admit this was somewhat fun. The cheers and laughter from the children as he handed out toys buoyed his spirits. Or maybe that was just the effect of Carli's infectious laugh as she walked by his side. He even attempted a lame "Ho-ho-ho" once or twice. Eventually, the onslaught of children approaching them slowed to a steady trickle, with a single child here and there. Good thing. His bag of toys was nearly empty.

"Aunt Carli!" Ray's exuberant voice rang behind them, and they both turned around as the boy ran up.

"Ray!" Carli bent and embraced her nephew. "Would you like to say hello to Santa?"

Ray's response was a knowing giggle. "That's not Santa! That's Justin!"

Carli gave a frantic look around and put her

gloved finger to Ray's mouth. Luckily, no other kids were near them at the moment.

"Shh, you don't want to spoil it for the other kids."

"Okay."

"But how did you know?" Carli asked the child as Justin crouched to give him a fist bump.

Ray shrugged as if it should be obvious. "Prolly 'cause his eyes. But mostly 'cause I know him. He's my friend."

"I see."

"And he's your boyfriend!" Ray added, nearly shouting this time as he clearly thought this was a hilarious thing to say.

Justin's eyes met Carli's over Ray's head. A surge of emotion shot through him. Her nose had gone a deep cherry-red in the cold. She wore a fuzzy elf's hat on top of her head with a small bell at the end. Her ears were adorned with the same snowman earrings she'd worn the night of her office party. The whole look was meant to appear whimsical and fun in the spirit of Christmas.

He didn't think any woman had ever looked more strikingly beautiful.

"You're right," Carli answered her nephew. "He is my boyfriend."

EPILOGUE

One year later

JUSTIN SCANNED THE large and ever-growing crowd in front of him. All of Westerson appeared to be here. He'd been an official resident for just under a year now, and it never ceased to amaze him the degree of loyalty the people of this town had for each other.

How he'd managed to snare one of their own as his fiancée he would never fully grasp. But he knew better than to ever take it for granted.

The object of his thoughts approached him from the side of the dais. "It's time to cut the ribbon," Carli prompted.

Mr. Freider came to stand next to her. He would be the one doing the actual cutting. After having managed the store for over two decades, and how hard the man had worked to bring the new version to fruition, he more than deserved the honor.

James and Noelle stood ready behind them near the podium. They'd flown in two days ago for the grand opening of the new and improved Hammond's Toys Cape store. A project that had been a year in the making.

"Ready?" he asked her.

"I think so. Funny, I know everyone here quite well. But I'm still nervous to speak in front of all these people."

"You'll do great," he assured her.

Carli leaned into the microphone and cleared her throat. "Thank you everyone for coming," she began. "We are so excited to unveil the new Hammond's Toys Cape store. Although the name has not changed, a lot inside the store has. For those of you who haven't had a chance to read the write-up in the *Westerson Eagle* or haven't otherwise heard, Hammond's now is so much more than a toy store. It's been expanded to include a teen center, an arts and crafts area, which will offer weekly lessons, as well as a state-of-the-art arcade. And so much more in the way of seasonal activities depending on the time of year." She gave him a smile that shot pleasure through his chest, then took a deep breath. "I can't tell you how proud it makes me to tell you that all this was the brainchild of my fiancé, Justin Hammond." She held her hand out toward him.

Justin's turned to the audience and took a mock bow. "That was the easy part," he yelled toward the crowd. As was the financing. Justin had found willing investors in a relatively short period of time once he explained his vision. The store was such a central point of the town, it only made sense to have it offer more reasons for the customers to visit and more for them to do once they got there. All those new attractions Carli mentioned would not only bring in their own revenue, they'd increase traffic to the actual toy store—resulting in higher sales.

Carli continued. "And now, without further delay, we would like to welcome you to the new Hammond's."

Cheers and raucous clapping erupted before she even finished the sentence. Once the applause died down, the five of them watched as Mr. Freider handled the comically large scissors to cut the wide red ribbon. Two newly hired employees dressed as elves pulled the double doors open to let the still cheering crowd into the renovated store.

His brother came to give him an enthusiastic handshake. "Well, done, man."

"Thanks." It was taking a while, but they were slowly starting to get to know each other. Bonding over the two women in their lives played no small role in their growing relationship.

"I can't tell you how much Noelle appreciates Carli's gesture," James told him, his gaze traveling to where the two ladies stood chatting by the doors. "She's really looking forward to being a bridesmaid."

What was one more? Justin thought. At this rate they were going to have the largest bridal party ever heard of. Not that he was complaining. Carli Tynan deserved to have the wedding she wanted, down to every detail. "I'm glad they're growing so close."

Right on cue, the two women shared a laugh at something Carli had said. Justin and James went to join them.

"You did great," he told her as James and Noelle entered the store.

"I'm glad that part's over," she replied. "Now

we can finally start planning for the other big event."

"Oh? I'm not exactly sure what you might be referring to. There's a lot happening," he teased, and gave her a playful tap on the tip of the nose. She meant the wedding, of course.

"Very funny."

Justin pulled her to him and gave her a deep, lingering kiss. Something told him planning their nuptials was going to take just as much time and effort as opening the new store had. That's what happened when you had a family as large as the Tynans and everyone possessed input they had to share.

He wouldn't have it any other way.

The easiest decision by far had been picking the date. Twelve months from now, Justin would be walking his Christmas bride down the aisle.

He could hardly wait.

* * * * *

LET'S TALK
Romance

For exclusive extracts, competitions and special offers, find us online:

f facebook.com/millsandboon

⊙ @millsandboonuk

🐦 @millsandboon

Or get in touch on 0844 844 1351*

For all the latest titles coming soon, visit millsandboon.co.uk/nextmonth

*Calls cost 7p per minute plus your phone company's price per minute access charge

Want even more
ROMANCE?

Join our bookclub today!